When Clare walked into the party, she felt all eyes turn, and heard the sudden lapse in the conversation

Her cheeks flushed when she saw the heads of two women close together and heard one passing on the gossip. "Didn't you know? That's the girl Jack Straker had an affair with. And there's a child involved evidently. It was all in the papers."

Clare turned toward the door and found herself gazing at the one man she didn't want to see—Jack Straker. He looked toward her, his expression deeply sardonic. But Clare's chin came up, set and determined.

There was no way she was going to let Jack have a part in her son's life. Not after what he'd done....

SALLY WENTWORTH was born and raised in Hertfordshire, England, where she still lives, and started writing after attending an evening class course. She is married and has one son. There is always a novel on the bedside table, but she also does craftwork, plays bridge and is the president of a National Trust group. They go to the ballet and theater regularly and to open-air concerts in the summer. Sometimes she doesn't know how she finds the time to write!

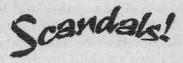

Have you heard the latest?
Get ready for the next outrageous Scandal

MISTRESS OF THE GROOM (#1918)
by
Susan Napier

All will be revealed in November 1997

SALLY WENTWORTH

A Very Public Affair

Harlequin Books

TORONTO • NEW YORK • LONDON
AMSTERDAM • PARIS • SYDNEY • HAMBURG
STOCKHOLM • ATHENS • TOKYO • MILAN
MADRID • WARSAW • BUDAPEST • AUCKLAND

ISBN 0-373-11912-7

A VERY PUBLIC AFFAIR

First North American Publication 1997.

CHAPTER ONE

THE house with its tree-framed lawns stood before her, but Clare felt no sense of familiarity, not even of *déjà vu*. She walked briskly up to the front door, turned the key in the lock and pushed it open. And it wasn't until she stepped into the hall and saw the black and white tiles that lined the floor, and the beautiful, graceful furniture, that memory came rushing back. She gave a gasp and stood transfixed. It had been six years ago, but the days that she and Jack Straker had been here together—the one night she had spent in his arms—were suddenly complete in her mind, vivid and alive. As was the agony that had followed.

Slowly Clare stepped inside the house, hardly glancing at the antiques she had come to value. In a trance, she walked up the stairs to the small bedroom she had used. The bed was still there, stripped now of its covers, but she could almost feel the force and strength of his hunger for her, the love and comfort she had given in return.

Her heart pounded in her ears as she stared down at the bed. Her breath came in gasping, unsteady sobs, and she didn't hear another car arrive or the door downstairs open, wasn't aware that there was anyone else in the house until she heard a man's voice call out, 'Hello, there. Miss Longman?'

She whirled with a sick feeling of terror. He

mustn't find her in this room. Running out onto the landing, Clare hardly glanced at the man standing in the hall. She knew it was Jack, would have known that deep voice anywhere. She even still heard it in her dreams, her nightmares. Quickly she went down the stairs to where he stood silhouetted by the light from the open door.

'Sorry I wasn't here to meet you,' he began. 'I'm afraid I got delayed on the motorway and...' For a moment Clare thought he wasn't going to recognise her, but then his voice faded as his eyes widened. 'Clare? My God! It *is* you.'

'I didn't know this was your house,' she said defensively. 'I never knew the address, where it was.'

'No, I suppose not.' Jack was still staring at her incredulously. 'You've changed so much. I hardly knew you.'

Avoiding his eyes, unable to even look at him directly, Clare moved past him towards the door and said hurriedly, 'You'll have to get someone else to do your valuation.'

Realising what she was doing, Jack reached out to catch her arm. 'But surely—'

A great fear filled her, a terror close to panic, and her voice rose. 'Don't you dare touch me!'

Jack gave an astonished laugh. 'But this is ridiculous. It was all so long ago, and—' He broke off, brought up short as she looked directly at him at last and he saw the vehement, naked fury in her eyes.

'Get out of my way!' Pushing past him, Clare ran outside to her car, pulling the door open and getting quickly inside.

Coming after her, he called out, 'Clare, please wait. Look, there's really no need—'

But she had started the engine and was already reversing to turn. She went to move forward again but had to brake sharply—Jack had moved to stand right in the middle of the driveway. His face looked hard, determined. 'I'm not going to let you leave like this, Clare.'

Putting her hand on the horn, she held it there, drowning out his words.

With an angry exclamation he came round to the side of the car, but Clare seized the opportunity and shot away, sending the car hurtling out of the driveway and down the lane. Her one thought was to find Toby and get away from here. Because Jack must never find him, never know that he existed. Her breath sobbing in her throat, Clare drove out onto the main road and tore down to the village.

Toby, her five-year-old son and the most precious thing in her life, was playing in the garden of the guest house where she'd booked a room. Grabbing him, desperately trying to keep her voice calm and not frighten him, she said, 'The job's fallen through. We've got to go. Now! We must pack quickly, quickly.'

'But, Mummy, we've only just—'

But she pulled him inside to their room and began to throw their things, which they'd unpacked only an hour ago, into the case. 'Come on. *Come on.*' She rushed him downstairs again and thrust some money into the hands of the astonished landlady. 'Sorry, something's come up. We won't be able to stay after all.'

Clare threw the case in the boot and jumped in the car. 'Do your safety belt up. Quickly, now, Toby.' The road south went past the entrance to the lane that led to the house, but there was nothing Clare could do about that. She put her foot down and drove as fast as she dared, desperate to get away.

A slow-moving delivery van blocked the way and there was a car coming from the opposite direction. As it passed Clare glanced across and saw that Jack was driving it. He saw her—and his eyes widened in astonishment as he saw Toby in the back!

MILLIONAIRE FIGHTS FOR ACCESS TO
LOVE-CHILD

Jack Straker, 35, the entrepreneur who has made a fortune out of his worldwide business empire, has found that money can't buy him what he wants most in the world—a son to carry on his name and inherit his vast fortune. Divorced and childless, with no sign of wishing to marry again, Straker looked set for a lonely future until chance took a hand and he met again a woman he had known some years ago—and found that she had borne him a son!

To his great disappointment, however, the child's mother, Miss Clare Longman, 25, has refused to allow the millionaire near the boy. It's rumoured she even denied the relationship at first, until it was found that she'd entered Straker's name on the birth certificate. The boy, known as Toby Longman, is five years old and a pupil at an exclusive school in London, where he lives with his mother.

Jack Straker comes from a working-class background but showed great business skills from an early age, starting his first company when still at school and running that and two more while attending university, where he attained an honours degree. Often called 'the man with the golden touch', every enterprise that Straker undertakes seems to pay off. But will he win through this time? He has been forced to go to law to gain access to his son, but the boy's mother is said to be fighting him all the way.

What happened between the two to make the lady so against him neither will say. Maybe it's because Miss Longman is from an upper-class background;

her father—who along with her mother was killed in an accident soon after she was born—was a Colonel in the Guards. It would be intriguing to find out! We await the outcome of the lawsuit with interest and wish Straker—a well-known philanthropist—every success.

CHAPTER TWO

WHEN Clare walked into the room she felt all the eyes turn on her, heard the sudden lapse in the conversation. Chin high, she resolutely ignored it and walked up to the director of the auction house.

'Clare. So pleased you were able to come.' He shook her hand, his manner pleasant enough, but she noticed the speculative look in his eyes. She encountered the same look, or something very near it, on the faces of the other people who were gathered in the large room, people she had previously regarded as friends and colleagues. But now, since that damning piece about her in all the tabloids, their manner towards her had subtly changed—especially that of the men.

It had taken some courage to come tonight. Perhaps it would have been easier if it had just been people she knew, but this evening the auction house was sponsoring a major charity auction in aid of a London hospital for children. As one of their leading experts on art deco and art nouveau, Clare was expected to attend, and it would have been cowardice not to come. So, much as she would have liked to bury herself at home, Clare had put on her newest cocktail dress, stitched a smile on her face and here she was. Let them talk about her. So what? She could take it. But she was furious on Toby's behalf; already he was being teased at school about that damn lawsuit.

She took a glass of champagne and mingled with her fellow experts, trying to keep her manner as calm and natural as she could. But half an hour later the double doors of the salon were thrown open and the first of the guests arrived: the organisers of the occasion, rich society women and their husbands. They were followed by celebrities from all walks of life: the theatre, business, politics—everyone who wanted to see and be seen in this exclusive circle. As one of the hosts, Clare was kept busy, mingling with the guests, thanking those who had made donations to the charity, ignoring the small, knowing smiles when people recognised her. But her cheeks flushed when she saw the heads of two women close together and heard one passing on the gossip. 'Didn't you know? That's the girl Jack Straker had an affair with. And there's a child involved, evidently. It was in all the papers.'

Quickly Clare moved away, cursing her bad luck. There had been no real reason—except for her terror-stricken reaction—for Jack to suspect about Toby from that one glimpse he'd had of him in the car a couple of months ago. But he had. And it had taken him no time at all to track her down, and then look up Toby's birth certificate. But when he'd tried to contact her she'd returned none of his phone calls, hadn't answered his letters and had refused to let him in when he had called at the flat. But then he'd brought the lawsuit, so she'd had to take notice of that.

Clare turned towards the door. She'd done enough; no one would notice if she left now. A newcomer had arrived and she found herself gazing at the one man she didn't want to see—at Jack Straker. He took a purposeful step towards her but Clare quickly went to join a small group gathered round the most famous guest, a minor royal. The director good-naturedly presented her, and Clare took good care to stay within the group until the auction started a short time later and everyone went to their seats.

She sat on a spare chair at the end of a row, so that Jack had no chance of coming near her. Already people had noticed that he was there too, and were nudging their friends, whispering the news. Not that they were interested in Clare particularly; she was a comparatively small fish in a big pool. But Jack was famous—a shark who could devour every other fish for breakfast. Glancing out of the corner of her eye, Clare saw him take a seat on the other side of the room. He looked towards her, his expression deeply sardonic, and she hastily shifted her gaze to the front—but her chin came up, set and determined. There was no way she was going to let Jack have a part in Toby's life. Not after the way he'd treated her, used her.

The auction began and her thoughts drifted, away from that warm room with its bejewelled women and evening-suited men, back to the coldest winter's night she'd ever known...

CHAPTER THREE

THE car that paused at the road junction was big and sleek, silver-grey in colour beneath the street lights. It made a statement that was easy to read: whoever drove a car like this had to be successful, rich, a winner. Huddled in a shop doorway and shivering with cold, Clare—hopeless, completely broke, a loser—raised tired lids to glance at it, deeply envying the mobile cocoon of warmth and luxury on this freezing winter's night.

The lights changed to green and the car drove on, but turned into the courtyard of a block of flats just a few yards down the street on the opposite side. Watching, Clare saw the car pull up at the entrance and a man get out. He seemed in a great hurry, almost running through the doorway. He didn't even bother to shut the car door properly. Such casual disregard held Clare's attention. She waited for the man to come out again, her eyes fixed on the car, her whole mind consumed with the thought of the warmth inside it.

Slowly she dragged herself to her feet and as if drawn by an invisible but powerful magnet crossed the road towards the flats. Once out of the shelter of the doorway the icy blast of the wind caught her, made her gasp at its fierceness and brought tears that ran like icicles down her cheeks. Reaching the other side, Clare peered through the ornate iron railings that surrounded the block. The man still hadn't come out and the car door was definitely open a couple of inches. She glanced round to see if anyone was watching, but it was almost one in the morning and the street was empty. Even the London traffic had ceased, everyone eager to get home on such a cold night.

For a moment longer she hesitated, but a gust of freezing wind chilled her to the marrow and sent her hurrying through the entrance, up to the car. A moment later her numb fingers had found the latch of the rear door and she slipped inside, pulling that and the driver's door closed behind her. Immediately the cold of the wind was gone, making her give a sob of heartfelt relief. The inside of the car was very dark, but the back seat was deep and padded. Clare felt something fabric under her hand and found it was a rug, large and thick and beautifully soft. With a sigh of sheer bliss she lay back on the seat, curled into it and pulled the rug completely over herself.

The car must be new; she could smell the richness of the leather upholstery, catch the unmistakable hessian and wool smell of new carpet. But most of all she felt the warmth that still lingered. It was so long since she'd been warm. The winter had been so severe and she'd been cold for so long that it was almost impossible to remember what it had been like to be warm all the time, for it to be so commonplace that she hadn't even thought about it.

Clare's thoughts drifted, her tired brain unable to concentrate, and she fell asleep.

It was twenty minutes later before Jack Straker came out to the car. He had changed from the evening suit he'd been wearing when the phone call came and now had on jeans and a sweater, clothes more comfortable for the long drive north. He put his suitcase in the boot and threw his camel overcoat into the back, his movements brisk, compelled by the urgency in the voice of his father's neighbour. Flu, she'd said, but his father hadn't let her call him. Now pneumonia had set in and he wasn't getting better, was not responding to treatment. She was worried, but now her own family had gone down with the flu virus, giving her no time to spare for her elderly neighbour, and the old man refused to go into hospital.

He would, Jack thought. Such obstinacy was typical of his father. It was what had made him insist, when he'd retired from business, on going to live in a remote area of the Lake District so that he could devote his life to the fishing that he loved.

The grimness in Jack's lean face softened as he thought of his father. They didn't see each other often. They were both men of independent spirit—his father because that was the way he wanted to be, and Jack because that was the way he'd been brought up—but the bond between them still went deep. Jack's mother was dead, had died many years ago, and his father had shown no inclination to remarry, either out of love or the need for companionship. He was a man who could be perfectly content in his own company, and he had managed very competently until this illness had struck him down.

The unexpectedness of the neighbour's emergency call had been a shock, especially coming as it had when he'd been at a nightclub after an evening spent at the opera. Reaching the motorway that ringed London, Jack put his foot down and headed north.

* * *

Having the coat thrown over her had startled Clare
out of her sleep. She'd woken in fright, thinking that
she was still in the shop doorway and that she was
being attacked. But then the car had started to move
and she'd remembered where she was. For a moment
she was petrified that she'd been seen, but then realised that she couldn't have been or the driver would
have thrown her out. Clare hazily thought that she
ought to let the driver know she was there, or heaven
knew where she might end up. But the car was so
warm, and the heavy overcoat had made her cosier
still. She thought about it, and while she was still
thinking fell deeply asleep again.

The big car ate up the miles, its engine the soft purr
of a well-bred cat. Jack turned on the radio to a clas-
sical music channel but kept it low. The programme
was interrupted from time to time by traffic bulletins
which spoke of freezing temperatures and the threat
of snow as he went ever further north. Two hours out
of London he pulled off the motorway into a service
area, where he filled the car up with petrol then went
into the café where he bought a flask of coffee and a
couple of rolls.

Clare didn't wake then, but she did when Jack
stopped again some time later and took a drink from
the flask. It was the aroma of the coffee that got to
her, filtering through the covers and making her in-
sides ache with hunger. Gently, very slowly, she
pulled the cover from around her face. The smell of
the coffee was immediately stronger, making her
throat tighten with thirst. She thought she'd die for a
cup, for just a mouthful, a taste. Then she heard him
unwrap a roll and smelt the ham that filled it, had to

push her hand in her mouth and bite on it to stop herself crying out, the hunger in her belly a physical pain.

It was a relief when the car started off again and there was just the sound of music and the smell of the leather seats. She saw white wisps hitting the windows and knew that it was snowing. With a great shiver, Clare pulled the car rug close again. Fleetingly she wondered about the driver. She could see it was a man, but that was about all. His head was mostly hidden by the head rest, and all she could see of him was a wide pair of shoulders and the top of his dark head faintly outlined by the lights on the dashboard. Impossible to tell any more of him, but she had the impression that he was young. Was that good or bad? And how would he react when he found her, when they arrived at wherever he was heading?

Clare found she didn't much care—about any of it. Things could hardly get worse for her than they were already, so what was the point of worrying? At least at the moment she was warm and comfortable, and she decided just to be thankful for that and to hell with the rest. So she slept again as the car continued on through the night—more slowly now in the bad conditions.

It was almost seven in the morning and the sky had lightened, but Jack still needed his headlights; the snow was becoming much heavier as the wipers incessantly cleared it from the windscreen. He had left the main road behind and the snow was worse on these minor roads, piling into drifts so that he had to use all his concentration. Coming to a crossroads,

Jack slowed to peer at the signpost but was unable to read it. Pulling into the side, he looked at the map but realised it was no good; he would have to go and clear the damn sign.

Opening the door of the car, he felt the cold hit him. He stretched his shoulders, easing his aching back muscles, then opened the rear door and reached in for his overcoat. He pulled it out. Beneath it the rumpled car rug moved! Jack stared, then reached in and yanked the rug away to reveal the figure lying on the seat.

'What the heck? How the hell did you get in there?' And, grabbing hold of an enveloping anorak, he dragged the person out of the car.

Coming to with a shock, Clare almost fell as he pulled her roughly out into the road. Her legs had gone stiff from being curled up for so long and she could hardly stand, making her stumble and catch hold of him to steady herself. Immediately Jack pushed her away and then gave her a violent shake, his face full of anger and distaste.

'Who are you? When did you get in the car?' Clare didn't answer and he gave her another rough shake. The hood of the anorak fell off and her hair, long and dark, tumbled about her head. 'Good grief! A girl.'

For a moment they stood in the road, the snow swirling about them as they stared at each other. Clare, looking at him in nervous alarm, saw that Jack was tall and that she'd been right in thinking him young—he looked to be in his late twenties, his hair almost as dark as her own. His eyes full of startled anger, he said again, 'Who are you? How did you get in the car?'

A snowflake settled on her lashes and Clare lifted her hand to wipe it away, then shivered and said, 'Please—I'm cold.'

Jack hesitated, then gave a curse and strode over to clear the sign. Taking this as an acceptance of her being there, Clare quickly got back into the car. He joined her a minute later, closing the door to keep out the cold, then looked at her over the back of his seat. 'Where did you get in—at the petrol station?'

Clare nodded, not seeing any point in telling him she'd been there all the way from London.

'Damn! I haven't got time to take you all the way back there. Where do you live?' She didn't speak and he said exasperatedly, 'Haven't you got a tongue in your head? Where do you live?'

'I—I don't live anywhere.'

His eyebrows rose, then he frowned. 'I suppose you've run away from home.' Again Clare didn't speak and he thumped his clenched fist against the seat in annoyance. 'What the hell am I going to do with you?'

Terrified that he might kick her out into the snow, Clare sat very still, her hazel eyes, large with apprehension, fixed on his face.

As if reading her thoughts, Jack said, 'I ought to throw you out. I would too, if it wasn't so damn cold.' Making up his mind, he turned away and put on his safety belt, started the car and began to drive again. 'Don't think that I'm letting you get away with this. As soon as I possibly can I'm going to hand you over to the police and let them deal with you.'

With a great inner sigh of relief Clare settled back in the seat, but stayed sitting up, just pulling the rug around her again. Looking out of the windows, she could see no houses anywhere, just expanses of open fields and sometimes a few trees, their branches already white with snow. The man, she could see, was giving all his attention to his driving. Once the car skidded and it looked as if they were headed for a ditch, but he quickly straightened it, then gave a grunt of satisfaction as he saw a farmhouse and turned up the lane that ran along the side of it. The lane was short—about half a mile—then they came to another house, a smaller one, built of grey stone and with a copse of fir trees to the side. There was another car parked outside.

'Stay here,' the driver ordered, and didn't even glance at Clare as he hurried to the house.

The door was unlocked. Jack pushed it open and, seeing the landing light was on, ran upstairs. 'Mrs Murray?'

She was in his father's room, and turned with a great look of relief. 'Thank goodness you've come. The doctor's been and he's left some medicine.' Already she was reaching for her coat.

Glancing at the bed, Jack saw his father was sleeping. They went out on the landing before he said, 'How is he?'

She shook her head. 'I'm sorry—he's bad. Here, I've written down the doctor's number. He'll be able to tell you more than I can, although you might have trouble getting him; everyone around seems to be down with this flu.'

'You'll be wanting to get back to your family. How are they?'

'Oh, they're young and strong; *they'll* recover.' She

stopped short and flushed a little. And Jack, seeing it, suddenly realised with a sick feeling of shock what she was afraid to tell him.

'Is he so ill?' he said faintly, hoping against hope that she would deny it. But she gave a brief nod and went ahead of him down the stairs. 'I'll drive you home,' he said mechanically, his brain trying to come to terms with it but refusing to accept such terrible news.

'No, I have the car.' Mrs Murray looked out of the window. 'It's a good job you got here when you did; the lane soon gets blocked with snow and my husband's too ill to get the tractor out to clear it.'

She left him, and Jack went back to his father's room. He sat by the bed and took hold of his father's limp hand. For the first time he realised how aged the man looked. He was an old man, but Jack had never realised it before. His skin was very white and his breathing was laboured, unnatural. Jack sat beside him, his thoughts full of regret and sadness, and it was a long time before he remembered the girl in the car.

Clare saw the woman hurry out of the house and the car drive away. She waited for the man to come back, peering out through the ever-thickening snow. Now that the engine was turned off the car began to get cold again. And she was hungry, so hungry. Still the man didn't come back. At last, driven by hunger and by the warmth and shelter that the house promised, Clare got out of the car, gasping as the wind cut into her and the snow covered her shoes. Hurrying to the door, she went to knock, then hesitated and tried the knob. The door opened and she went quickly inside, afraid of making the man angry again but too cold and hungry not to risk it.

Closing the door, she looked apprehensively round, expecting any moment to have someone come up and demand to know what she was doing there. But the hall, with its black and white chequered floor, was empty. Fleetingly Clare noticed that it held the weirdest furniture and ornaments she'd ever seen, but then she saw an open door at the end of the passage from which came the smell of something cooking—a rich, savoury smell that had her through the door and into the kitchen in two seconds flat.

The delicious smell came from a large pan that simmered on the range. Broth? Stew? Soup? Hardly able to control the shaking eagerness of her hands, Clare found a bowl and spooned a large helping into it. She was so starved that she had eaten three helpings before she even bothered to look about her. The kitchen was large, well-lit, and beautifully warm. Again the furniture seemed different—it wasn't just square and utilitarian, there were curves and flowing lines, and the chairs round the table had very high backs, high enough to lean her head against. There was a big dresser against one wall and on its shelves was lots of china in unusual shapes and in bright, bold colours: orange, yellow and vivid blue. The vibrant colours added to the warmth and welcome of the room, and brought a smile to her pale cheeks.

She glanced down at the bowl she'd been using and guiltily went to look in the pan. It was only a quarter full now. Clare gulped, wondering if she'd eaten most of the food intended for a whole family. She began to wonder, too, where the car driver had got to—but just then heard a door closing somewhere, and then rapid footsteps coming down the stairs. Nervously she went out into the hall.

Jack saw her as he came round the bend in the stairs, and stopped short in surprise. He had hardly taken her in before and was too full of shock over his father to do so now. All he knew was that the girl was a worry, an inconvenience he definitely didn't want, especially now. Annoyance making his voice harsh, he said, 'I told you to wait in the car.'

'It was cold.'

He saw that she was still wearing the anorak, that it was dirty and stained, as were the jeans that had made him think at first that she was a boy. Jack's nose wrinkled a little in distaste as he came down into the hall. 'When did you run away?'

It was impossible to deny that she was a runaway, but Clare couldn't see why he had to know, so she didn't answer.

Jack sighed. 'Have you at least got a name?'

She hesitated, then said, 'It's Clare.'

He was surprised, expecting her—if she'd told him at all—to have a far more common name. But perhaps she'd made it up. Deciding that she had, his face hardened. 'Clare what?' he demanded brusquely.

Not liking his tone, Clare's chin came up a little. 'Smith,' she said shortly.

His eyes went to her face at that, and registered a pair of defiant hazel eyes. With an angry exclamation he went past her into the kitchen. 'You're going to have to say who you are some time, you know. If not to me, then to the police.' Noticing the bowl on the table, he said wryly, 'I see you made yourself at home.'

'I'm sorry. I was hungry.'

He glanced in the pan, then said, 'You may as well finish it off.'

Clare didn't argue, immediately coming to fill her bowl again, but she managed to say, 'Don't you want any? It's very good.'

'No. I'll just make myself some coffee.' He gave her an assessing look, surprised by the educated tones of her voice. He'd expected her to be from a different background. 'How old are you?'

'Twenty-two,' Clare lied.

Jack gave a short laugh. 'Do you really expect me to believe that?' He had picked up the kettle but turned with it in his hands to look at her. She was, he realised, very thin and pale, and there were dark shadows round her eyes. She looked like a Victorian waif, thrown out into the snow. Roughly he said, 'You look about fourteen.'

'I'm not!' Clare said indignantly. 'I'm twenty-two.' She caught his eyebrows rising disbelievingly. 'Well—twenty, anyway.' But that was still a lie because she was only just nineteen.

She took her bowl to the table and a few minutes later he came to sit opposite with his mug of coffee. 'You,' Jack said shortly, 'are a damn nuisance. My father is upstairs and he's...' He hesitated and found that he was unable to say 'dying,' so said instead, 'He's very ill, and I can't leave him. So I'll have to phone the nearest police station and ask them to come and collect you.' He saw her fingers tighten on the spoon, but she didn't speak or look at him. 'Of course,' he went on, 'it would make things a whole lot easier if you'd tell me who you are so that your parents could come instead. I'm sure they must be terribly worried about you and—'

'I haven't any parents,' Clare said shortly.

Jack looked at her set face, wondering if she was lying again. 'Well, there must be someone who—'

'There isn't.'

He became exasperated. 'Look, I haven't got time to play games. It's your parents, guardian, or whatever—or the police. Which is it to be?'

Clare raised a strained face to look at him. 'The police won't want to know. I'm over-age and I have the right to lead whatever kind of life I want, wherever I want. They can't make me go back.'

'Well, at least you've admitted that there is somewhere for you to go back to,' Jack pounced. He stood up, fretting to get back to his father's side. 'And you're certainly not staying here.'

Going out to the car, he brought in his suitcase and overcoat. And his mobile phone, knowing that his father had never allowed a phone to be installed in the house—that or a television set. Dumping his case on the floor in the hall, Jack went into his father's book-lined study and called the number that Mrs Murray had left for him. There was some delay, but eventually he was connected with the local doctor. The doctor went into much greater detail but in the end the news was just the same: his father was dying; there was nothing more they could do for him.

'He knows; he made me tell him when I wanted him to go into hospital,' the doctor told Jack. 'But he said he wanted to die in his own home.'

'Is he in pain?'

'No. The medication I've left for him will remedy that. It's just a matter of time.'

His voice thin and strangled, not sounding at all like his own, Jack said, 'How long?'

'It's hard to say. A few days. Perhaps a week. I'll come as often as I can, but I've a flu epidemic on my hands. Will you be staying with him, or do you want me to try and get a nurse?'

'No, that won't be necessary; I'll be here as long as he needs me.'

He gave the doctor his mobile number then rang off. For a long moment he just sat staring at the wall, then roused himself and called the local police. They could do nothing about the girl today, they said when he explained the position. Half their men were down with the flu. They advised him to just send her on her way.

'It's snowing outside,' Jack pointed out.

He could almost hear the shrug in the policeman's voice. 'Unless you want to bring charges against her for breaking into your car, there's not a lot we can do except try and persuade her to go home. Has she given you her name? We could look on the missing-persons file and see if we can find an address for her.'

With inner anger, Jack told them to just come and collect the girl as soon as possible.

Going back into the kitchen, he found Clare washing out the now empty pan. She had taken off the anorak but it was impossible to tell what sort of figure she had as she seemed to be wearing several layers of sweaters. She turned her smudged, green-flecked eyes to look at him apprehensively. At any other time

Jack might have felt some sympathy, if not pity for her. But not now; his thoughts were too full of the days ahead and taking care of his father.

'You'll have to stay here until tomorrow,' he said abruptly. 'The police can't come for you until the morning.'

Clare relaxed a little, but then thought that maybe her troubles weren't over—she would be alone here with this man. But no, almost at once she realised that she had nothing to fear. He was too much preoccupied with his sick father to even think about her in that way.

'Come with me and I'll show you where you can sleep.' She followed him up the stairs. The banister rails were in that same flowing style, like graceful lilies. When they reached the corridor at the top he pointed out his father's room. 'I'll take the one next door.' He opened another door further down. 'I suppose you'd better have this room. You'll have to make the bed up. There's blankets and things in that cupboard on the landing. And the bathroom's over there.'

He turned to go to his father's room, but Clare said quickly, 'Please—can I have a bath?'

'Yes, of course.' He looked surprised that she'd asked.

'And—and you know my name, but I don't know yours.'

He gave a curt laugh. 'I know the name you've chosen to tell me, you mean.'

Having slept in the car for several hours, and feeling full of good food, warm for the first time in weeks, and knowing that she had somewhere to stay for the night, Clare was able to say lightly, 'A new life deserves a new name.'

His left eyebrow rose. 'Smith? Surely you could do better than that?'

She smiled a little and he saw with surprise that there was a trace of beauty in her thin features. Somehow this made him angrier, and he said harshly, 'My name's Straker, Jack Straker. Look, I may be stuck with you till tomorrow but I shall expect you to keep out of the way. I haven't got time to worry about you. Understand?'

Her face flushed at the obvious rebuff and she said stiffly, 'Yes. I'm sorry.'

He nodded and went on his way.

Jack's father might have been anti-telephones but he had utilised modern technology to take care of his creature comforts; the house was centrally heated and there was a very efficient plumbing and water-heating system. Clare must have stayed in the bath for over a couple of hours, washing her hair, absolutely wallowing in the pleasure of soaking in all that lovely hot water.

Since she'd left what Jack had called her 'home'— but which she'd thought of as purgatory—she'd tried to keep herself clean, washing herself in public ladies' cloakrooms after she'd had to leave the cheap hotel where she'd stayed until her money had run out. She'd been able to wash and change her clothes then, too, because she'd carried a backpack crammed with her belongings. But, to her despair, it had been stolen one night as she'd lain asleep on a park bench and since then she'd had nothing but the clothes she was wearing.

Reluctant to put her beautifully clean body back into them, Clare found a towelling robe hanging on the bathroom door and put that on instead. Her hair she towelled as dry as possible, but she had nothing to brush it with so it had to stay a dark, tangled mass about her head. Bare footed, she picked up all her clothes and took them downstairs to the kitchen, then thrust the whole lot into the washing machine and switched it on. Checking the cupboards and freezer, she found that the house was well-stocked with food, so, still feeling guilty at having eaten all the stew, she set about cooking a meal.

Upstairs, old Mr Straker woke at last. When he saw Jack he smiled and reached for his hand. Jack gripped it tightly. They didn't speak; there was no need for words. They both knew why he had come and that this would be their last time together.

The kitchen seemed to buzz with activity. When Jack went down there to get his father some water he found Clare—still in the bathrobe—busily blending soup, the tumble-dryer turning, pans simmering on the stove. 'I thought you'd be hungry by now,' she explained, her face a little flushed. 'So I made some lunch. I'll go upstairs while you eat it,' she added hastily, remembering she was supposed to keep out of his way.

Jack almost did a double take, she looked so different. With her hair all mussed like that, and the colour in her cheeks, she looked startlingly attractive, almost beautiful. Taken aback, unprepared for her to look anything like human, let alone this, all he could find to say was, 'You haven't got any shoes on.'

'I've only got the one pair, and they're really grotty.'

'What about your clothes?'

She pointed to the tumble-dryer.

'Are they all you've got?'

Clare's face hardened a little. Of course they were all she'd darn well got! Couldn't he see that? Acidly she said, 'If I'd known I was coming to stay I'd have brought a suitcase full of designer clothes with me.'

Immediately after she'd said it she wished she hadn't; after all, it wasn't his fault that she'd ended up here and been dumped on him like this. Expecting him to get mad, she was completely surprised when Jack gave a rough laugh. He didn't speak, but went away and came back with a thick pair of woollen socks that he held out to her. 'My dad uses these when he goes hill walking. They should keep your feet warm.'

Slowly Clare walked over to take them. It was such a small thing, probably meant nothing to him, but it was a long time since anyone had shown her any kindness and it brought silly tears to her eyes. 'Thanks,' she said huskily as she took them.

Shrugging, he turned to get some water.

'I'm making some soup. Do you think your father might like some?' Clare ventured.

'Let's give it a try.'

Jack went upstairs carrying a tray, leaving Clare to eat alone, and he didn't come down again until an hour or so later for his own lunch, by which time her clothes were dry and Clare had dressed again.

She left him alone to eat it, spending the time looking round the house. Every room seemed to be filled with the unusual furniture and ornaments, and the more she looked at it the more it grew on her. She was examining a pretty lamp, shaped like three intertwining tulips, in what was evidently the sitting-room, when Jack came in.

'I've never seen furniture like this before,' she explained.

'It's art deco and art nouveau,' Jack said casually. 'My father has a passion for it. He's been collecting it most of his life.' He saw her puzzled look and said, 'There are books galore on it in the study, if you're interested.'

Jack went back upstairs, dismissing the girl from his mind. His father woke again for a while and he gave him his medicine, but soon he was asleep, his breathing laboured, painful. Jack brought the pillows and duvet from the room that Mrs Murray had got ready for him, made up a bed on the settee in the old man's room and spent the night there in lonely vigil.

In the morning his phone rang. It was Mrs Murray, saying that the lane was blocked with snow and she couldn't get through to the house. Later the police rang and said the main road was blocked, too; they didn't know when they could get there. So he was stuck with Clare indefinitely.

He hadn't slept much; the settee was too short for his six feet two inches. And the previous night there had been the long drive to get here. He was dog-tired but full of deep anger against the fate that had done this to his father, against the girl for hiding in his car, definitely against the snow and even—God help him—because his father hadn't taken better care of himself and had allowed himself to become so ill.

The days stretched endlessly into one another. The skies were so dark outside that Jack sometimes didn't know whether it was day or night. He slept only when his father did—and that was only lightly, continuously waking to listen again to the old man's agonised breathing. Sometimes he was a little better and managed to talk, although it was obvious that it pained him. Those moments were precious to Jack, making up for many wasted opportunities, for enforced separations. The doctor phoned every day, but there was little help or advice he could give. The roads were still blocked, but he had left plenty of medication; there was nothing else he could do.

At least Jack didn't have to worry about preparing food; Clare had taken it on herself to do that, to do the washing and even clean the house. When Jack came downstairs he would find her working away, apparently quite happily, or else curled up in the armchair in the kitchen, deep in one of his father's books on art nouveau. They didn't talk much; he wasn't interested in her, but he was grateful that she had taken so many niggling worries off his shoulders.

One morning, when they'd been there nearly a week, Clare came into the kitchen to clear away after his breakfast and found him still there, slumped in the armchair and deeply asleep. She had always been intimidated by him, but he looked so vulnerable now.

She moved to look at him, at the strong, lean face with its square chin, wide forehead and straight dark brows. His features were clean-cut, finely drawn, but his good looks weren't the first thing that you noticed about him—it was his determination and self-assurance that came across most strongly. You got the impression he would be irritated at being liked for his looks; it was his personality that was all-important.

Studying him, Clare thought that if she had met him in other circumstances she would have been attracted by him, the way young girls are often attracted by the hint of ruthlessness and power in a man.

She thought she'd better wake him, and said, 'Mr Straker.' Then, more loudly, 'Mr Straker.' He didn't even blink, he was so soundly asleep. She hesitated, but then decided to let him sleep on and instead went upstairs to the invalid's room.

It was the first time she'd seen Jack's father, and Clare knew at once that he was dying. Her grandmother had looked just like that, so pale and sunken, when Clare had been taken to say goodbye to her before she'd died, ten years ago now. Sitting down in the chair where Jack had spent so many hours, she quietly kept watch while he slept.

It was over an hour before Jack woke, doing so with a start. Immediately he ran upstairs and was furious when he saw Clare by his father's bed. Grabbing hold of her arm, he propelled her outside onto the landing. 'Why were you with him?'

'You were asleep, so—'

'Did he call out? Why didn't you wake me?'

'You were so tired. I thought—'

'Who the hell asked you to think?' Jack snarled.

'You keep out of there. I don't want him waking to find some stranger with him instead of me. Is that clear?'

'Perfectly clear,' Clare answered shortly, her colour rising. Tugging her arm free, she headed towards the stairs.

Watching her, seeing the injured set of her shoulders, Jack gave an inner groan. 'Look, I didn't mean...' But she was already running down the stairs.

The sleep had done him little good; for the rest of that day he kept dozing in the chair and jerking awake. In the afternoon his father's breathing seemed to have eased a little and Jack looked at him hopefully, wondering if, against all the odds, he would recover. Towards evening, hardly able to keep his eyes open, Jack went down to the kitchen to make himself a drink. Clare, reading in her room, heard him go, and return some ten minutes later. Then came the most terrible sound—a great cry of anguish followed by, 'No! No! Oh, God, no!'

Leaping up, she ran out onto the landing. Jack came slowly out of his father's room, his face completely white and rigid with shock.

'What is it? What's happ—?' Clare suddenly realised, and her heart filled with sympathy for Jack.

His voice slurred, unnatural, he said, 'He's dead.'

Clare reached out a tentative hand of comfort but he didn't even see it. Brushing past her, Jack went down the stairs and into the study where he'd left his mobile phone. Even though he had expected this, the shock was so great that his mind was refusing to really take in what had happened, to accept the finality of it. It was as if that part of his mind and all the emotions that it would evoke had been blanked off, and he was concentrating entirely on practical things. With a hand that visibly shook, Jack called the doctor and told him.

'There's a snowplough in the village now,' Jack was told. 'I'll get the driver to come up your lane and I'll follow with an ambulance. They've already cleared most of the road, so it shouldn't take too long.'

But it was over three hours before they heard a noise outside and saw the lights of the vehicles. Jack spent the time pacing the floor in the hall, just striding up and down, refusing to think, to feel, while Clare stayed quietly in the kitchen out of the way, sensing that he needed to be alone. The doctor, looking tired out, dealt quickly with the formalities. Old Mr Straker's body was taken away in the ambulance and then Jack and Clare were alone again in the silent house.

Jack had gone up with the doctor to his father's room and hadn't come down. After a while Clare went upstairs and got ready for bed, but as she came out of the bathroom she heard what sounded like a groan, and stood irresolutely on the landing.

Inside the room Jack stared down at the empty bed, the mental padlocks he had put on his mind slowly dissolving as he at last began to accept his father's death. And, because he had held back his feelings with such iron will-power and determination for all these hours, his feelings completely overwhelmed him as he relaxed. He was consumed by a tidal wave of grief that robbed him of all self-control. He went out

of the room, staggering, holding onto the door jamb
as if his legs wouldn't support him.

Clare saw that his arm was up across his face and
he looked to be in deep distress. Going to him, she
took his arm and he leaned heavily on her. 'I wasn't
there!' he exclaimed brokenly, anger and guilt adding
to his grief. 'All these hours—and yet I wasn't there
when he went, when he needed me.' Swinging away
from her he leaned his head against the wall, beating
at it with his clenched fists. 'There was still so much
to say. I didn't even get to say goodbye to him.'

'Perhaps he didn't wake,' Clare soothed. She shut
the door of the room and tried to pull Jack away. He
let her lead him. His body was shaking not only from
grief but from utter exhaustion, she saw. 'You're so
tired; you must sleep now.'

The bed in his own room wasn't made up so she
guided him into hers. He was still muttering incoher-
ently and shaking his head from side to side in deep
grief, blaming himself for going downstairs. 'I
shouldn't have left him. I shouldn't have left him.'

'You weren't to know.'

She sat him on the bed and bent to pull off his
shoes, tried to push him back onto the pillow. But he
got agitatedly to his feet and strode up and down the
small room as if he were in a prison cell. Then
abruptly he sat down again, his head in his hands.

Words were a waste of time; it was too soon for
them, Clare realised. So she sat down next to him and
put comforting arms round his shoulders. His body
was shaking and for a while he couldn't control his
grief—the terrible pain of it, the dreadful fatigue that
left him without the strength to hide it.

Somehow it didn't feel strange, holding him like this. Jack was still virtually a stranger, and yet she knew exactly what he was going through—understood all the raw emotion that engulfed him. It didn't seem at all incongruous that her slight strength should support him, that he should lean against her while he went through these first terrible spasms of ache and loss.

Clare went on holding him for what seemed a long time, but eventually his trembling eased a little and he wiped the back of his hand across his eyes and lifted his head. Clare went to move away but he turned within her arms. His eyes, dark and still wide with shock, held hers. She was wearing just an old shirt that she'd found in a drawer, a man's, much too big for her and coming down to her knees. Jack, his face intense, reached out to touch it at the neck.

'This was his.'

'Yes.' She tried to say sorry, thinking that he was offended by it, but the words died in her throat as she looked into his eyes and began to understand even more.

Slowly he ran his fingers down over her breast. 'You're so alive,' he said huskily, his voice strained. 'So alive.'

Clare caught her breath at his touch. Instinctively she knew what he wanted—and why. His father's death had made him realise his own vulnerability, how precarious life was. He needed to be close—very close—to someone, to convince himself that life could go on. For a long moment she looked deeply into the intense grey eyes that held hers, then stood up and slowly lifted the shirt, pulled it over her head and stood before him in all the beauty of her naked youth.

Jack groaned as he looked at her, a sound almost of agony, then reached out a trembling hand to touch her waist, her thighs. 'Are you sure? Oh, God, are you sure?'

For answer she leant forward and placed her lips against his.

The trembling in his body was so strong that she could feel it even in this light touch. For a moment he just let her kiss him, but then Jack surged to his feet, his hand behind her head, his mouth taking hers now in urgent need. Still kissing her, making small, animal sounds against her mouth, he somehow dragged off his clothes until he, too, was naked. He touched her breasts and ran kisses down her throat as she arched her neck, wanting him now. Bending her back against his arm, he let his other hand run free over her, glorying in her living warmth, the velvet softness of her skin.

Jack's need for her was dreadful, the deepest hunger he'd ever known, an ache so bad that he could scarcely bear the pain of it. He needed to shut out the pictures in his mind, to experience the joy, the certainty of sexual fulfilment—to convince himself that life was still sweet. He needed it so badly that nothing else mattered, not conscience, convention, not even common sense.

In the young, pliant body in his arms he knew he would find solace, would assuage the devils of guilt and grief that haunted his mind. His hot, unsteady hands pulled her close to him so that he could hold her against his length, feel the heat of her. He heard her gasp when he put his hands low on her hips and held her against his growing manhood. That excited him unbearably. He wound his hand in her long dark hair and took her mouth again, letting passion have free rein. She was excited now, he could feel it in the heat of her skin, hear it in her gasping breath. Her hands were on him, as eager as his own.

With a cry, Jack swung her onto the bed. Her hair spread like a fan across the whiteness of the pillow. He saw her face below him, her features sharpened by desire, but it was the heart of her he wanted—the one place where he could find the peace and fulfilment he craved. So he took her, took her in desperate, driven hunger. No tender act of love this, but a savage need for reassurance to overcome the primitive age-long fear of mortality. And as excitement came, engulfed him, Jack wanted to shout out that he was alive—alive!

He fell asleep almost at once and slept long and deeply, held in Clare's arms in the narrow bed. Some hours later he half woke, still too exhausted to be fully aware of his surroundings, but realised he was in bed and that the room was dark. He felt the woman beside him and without opening his eyes reached for her. She kissed him, murmured his name, used her hands and body to arouse him, then pushed him back and came over him, taking her own pleasure, her long cry of excitement filling the room.

When Jack finally woke it was to a feeling of immeasurable peace. He was alone in the room and sunshine, of all things, shafted through the window. For a little while he lay there, knowing that he had made love and savouring the wonderful feeling. But slowly, and then with sickening clarity, remembrance came. His father was dead—and he had taken Clare, the young girl who had foisted herself on him but nevertheless had had a right to be safe from him. At first he was appalled, not because he'd done such a thing with his father newly dead—the old man, he knew, would have been quite amused by it—but because he might have taken Clare against her will. But then he remembered that she had been a very eager participant and that guilt eased a little. But not his conscience. He should never have done it. There were no circumstances that justified what he'd done.

But Jack wasn't the type to brood on the past, on what couldn't be undone. Swiftly he got up, went to the bathroom and dressed, then ran downstairs.

Clare was in the kitchen. She was keyed up with excitement. Last night had been out of this world for her, a revelation of what sex, fantastic sex, could be like. She felt so good, so content and happy. She had never known that sex could make you feel like this— walking on air, wanting to laugh for no reason at all, to sing and dance around the room. Even if the sun hadn't been shining it would still have been the most wonderful day.

When Jack finally came in she ran to him, looking eagerly at his face, waiting for him to smile at her with the intimacy of shared knowledge. But he didn't take her in his arms as she wanted. Instead he put her gently aside. 'There are a lot of phone calls I ought to make.'

'Oh. Of course.' She stood back. He moved towards the door but she said impulsively, 'Jack?'

Half turning, he gave a crooked kind of grin. 'We'll talk later. In about half an hour. OK?'

She nodded, satisfied, and he went out to the study.

He was gone for longer than he'd said; it was almost an hour before he came back. She supposed that he had been informing other members of his family of his father's death, and she wondered how long it would be before the funeral would take place. Jack, she was sure, would stay on here until then, so they could still be alone here together. Excitement rose at the thought.

But this hope was immediately shattered when Jack returned and said, 'I've been in touch with other relatives; they'll be coming here as soon as they can.' He paused, then said heavily, 'About last night. I suppose I ought to apologise, but I'm afraid I'm not sorry that it happened. I needed you—and I'm pretty certain you needed me almost as much.' He didn't wait for her to speak, but went on, 'But the fact remains that I took advantage of you being here. For your sake I shouldn't have done that.' He shrugged. 'But I did, and I'm grateful that you were so—accommodating.' His grey eyes rested on her face. 'And I'd like to show my gratitude by giving you this. It should keep you while you sort yourself out.' And he held out a folded piece of paper.

Clare didn't take it. She could see it was a cheque. Anger flared through her. Her chair fell over as she sprung to her feet. 'What the hell do you think I am— a prostitute? I didn't do it for *money*!'

Jack, too, stood up and came round the table. Catching hold of her arm, he said forcefully, 'I know that. It isn't a payment.'

Clare laughed bitterly. 'What else would you call it?'

'It's just a token, a way of saying thanks. What other way do I have?'

There were a million ways, Clare thought. Like taking her in his arms and saying how wonderful it had been for him. He could have kissed her, smiled, said he wanted it to happen all over again. Now. Tomorrow. That she was important to him now. But all he'd said was that he'd needed her, she'd been there, available, and so he'd taken her. Used her, in other words, but was going to assuage his conscience by paying for it! Clare felt a great surge of humiliation, and what had been wonderful suddenly became tainted and dirty.

Her voice tight, Clare said, 'I'm leaving here. Now!'

Her pride and dignity astounded him. Jack had expected her to take the money with relief, if not with pleasure—not act as if he'd somehow defiled her by offering it. She was destitute, for heaven's sake, and he'd only wanted to help her, to show his gratitude in the most practical way possible. But maybe it was better this way. He didn't want her clinging round him, creating a scene when he asked her to leave, so he said shortly, 'I've already arranged for a taxi to collect you. The trains are running, so it will take you to the nearest mainline station.'

She stared at him, her face stony. 'You just can't wait to get rid of me, can you?'

Jack paused, his eyes on her face, seeing that her anger gave her beauty. He felt a terrible reluctance to hurt her, but he knew it had to be done. His voice expressionless, he said, 'One of the people who's on their way here, who will be arriving probably later today, is my wife.'

The train was almost empty. Clare sat next to the window, looking unseeingly out at the fleeing landscape, the snow gradually giving way to patchwork fields and bare-branched trees. Jack had given her money for the fare to London and she'd had to take it. And just now, in the pocket of her anorak, she'd found the cheque he'd tried to give her earlier. It was for an immense amount, enough to keep her for ages. She would have liked to just tear it up, but she'd be an utter fool to do that. She could have afforded that kind of gesture when she'd thought there was a chance of staying with him, but not now that he had finally kicked her out. Out of his bed, out of his life.

She felt hot tears sting her eyes, but somehow blinked them back. What else had she expected, for heaven's sake? He'd been bound to kick her out eventually, and if she'd hoped for something more then she'd been just kidding herself. She had to forget that night. Forget Jack Straker. It was time to start a new life for herself, and the easiest way to do that was to forget he even existed.

CHAPTER FOUR

THE auctioneer brought his hammer down for the last lot and Clare jerked back to an awareness of her surroundings. Hastily she joined in the applause when the amount raised was announced. People had been very generous; the charity had done well. She saw Jack walk over to one of the cashiers, a cheque in his hand, and fleetingly wondered what he had bought; she'd been too absorbed in her own thoughts to notice. But her main concern now was to leave as quickly as possible, before he had a chance to approach her again.

Already there was a queue at the cloakroom for coats. Clare stood in line, impatiently tapping her foot, and retrieved hers at last. She turned to hurry away but an old schoolfriend, Tanya Beresford, there with her husband Brian, stopped her and asked her to have lunch the following week. Clare accepted and got away as quickly as she could. But she was too late. Jack was waiting by the entrance, a coldly determined set to his face. When she saw him Clare stopped, then turned to go back inside.

'Running away again?' he said scathingly. 'You seem to make a habit of it.'

'What I do is no business of yours,' Clare retorted icily.

'But that's where you're wrong.' Stepping forward, he took her arm in a vice-like grip. 'It seems that you're very much my concern.' And he led her to where a big, chauffeur-driven car waited by the kerb. The driver opened the door and Jack pushed her inside.

'Do you always go around being this high-handed?' Clare demanded angrily, uncomfortably aware that some other guests had followed her out and had seen them get in the car. That little titbit would, she supposed bitterly, be in all the gossip columns tomorrow.

Jack pressed a button on the console beside his seat and a glass panel slid up between them and the driver. It was the first time he'd managed to get her alone and he'd meant to be reasonable, but all he could feel was anger at the way she'd deceived him. 'I have tried every way possible to talk to you,' he said shortly. 'If you persist in refusing then I'm left with no alternative.'

'But I don't want to talk to you. And I insist you stop this car and let me out.'

'You know I'm not going to, so why say it?'

Clare laughed acidly. 'Yes, I suppose it is too much to hope that you'd ever behave with any consideration for anyone other than your egotistical self.'

Her bitterness took him aback. Jack's eyes narrowed as he realised he had more to deal with here than he'd thought. After a moment he said, 'Have you eaten yet? How about going somewhere for supper?'

'No.'

'No to which?'

Clare turned on him, her eyes full of antagonism. 'No to anything and everything you say. I want nothing to do with you.'

Jack was not used to being talked to so rudely. His

lips thinned and he said, 'Isn't it a bit late for that?'

Clare flushed and turned away, not wanting to be reminded of the night she'd spent with him. She'd been trying not to look at him directly, but it was hard not to remember the powerful body that was under the immaculate evening-suit, a body perfect in its masculinity. Yet again she wondered about his ex-wife, why they'd divorced. But that was nothing to do with her; she had enough to concentrate on in keeping him away from Toby.

Jack was trying to work out how to play it. Her flushed cheeks told him that she was still sensitive about their lovemaking, which surprised him; it had been so long ago. And just for that one night. But maybe she was entitled to be sensitive as it had resulted in her having a child. His voice more gentle, he said, 'Why didn't you tell me about Toby?'

Her eyes, a beautiful hazel with green lights, he noticed, flashed fire at him again. 'Toby is nothing to do with you.'

'He is according to his birth certificate,' he replied evenly.

'You had no right to look that up, to go prying into my life.'

'And you had no right to keep his existence from me,' Jack returned shortly.

Clare hesitated, then thought that she would do anything to keep Toby away from him. So she said, 'Actually—what I put on the certificate wasn't true. I—I don't know who his real father is. There were a couple—a few men around at the time. But I had to give some name, so I just picked yours out of thin air. But he definitely *isn't* yours,' she added for good measure.

For a moment he was astonished that she could cheapen herself in this way, but then recognised it for the desperate try that it was. 'The dates fit,' he pointed out. 'And a blood test would prove whether or not I am his father.'

'I won't let you or anyone else touch my son,' Clare said fiercely.

'The law will insist on it.'

The car stopped in a traffic jam and the lights from a nearby shop filled the car. Jack saw that Clare was very tense, her face white and her hands clenched into tight fists. At his most persuasive, he said, 'I don't mean Toby any harm, you know.'

Raising her eyes to meet his, Clare said forcefully, 'You would ruin his life—as you ruined mine!'

The car moved on and, her heart full of resentment, Clare couldn't resist asking, 'What made you take so long to sell your father's old place?'

'I'm not selling it. I keep it as a holiday home. I was just having the contents valued for insurance purposes. I didn't specifically ask for you to do the valuation, if that's what you're thinking. I just asked the auction house to recommend an expert. If you remember,' he added with some irony, 'you never told me your real surname.'

So it was nemesis, Clare thought with deep chagrin. Just cruel fate that had caught up with her and dealt her yet another blow.

They didn't speak again until the car finally came to a standstill. With surprise Clare saw that they were outside her own building. But if he thought she was going to invite him in he was crazy. She went to get out of the car but the chauffeur was there first, opening the door for her. And, instead of getting out on his own side, Jack followed her closely and took hold of her arm again.

'Come back in an hour,' he instructed the driver.

Clare rounded on him. 'Look, I've already told you I want nothing to do with you. I'm not going to talk to you. If you insist on bringing this stupid lawsuit then I can't stop you, it seems. But I refuse to discuss it.'

'Well, that's a shame because I'm not leaving until we have. And we can talk either here or in your place—suit yourself.'

'If you don't let go of me I'll have you arrested for assault,' Clare threatened.

Jack shrugged. 'That should look good in the papers.'

Her face tightened at that and Jack could almost have felt sympathy for her if he hadn't been so determined to get what he wanted—and by now he didn't much care how. She'd had her chance to meet him on a reasonable level. He must have called, written and gone personally to her flat about thirty times, but she'd flatly refused to even listen. So now she must take the consequences.

The car drove away and for a few moments they were alone, gazing at each other, each determined not to give way. But then a couple of taxis drove into the forecourt, carrying other tenants of the flats. Taking instant advantage of it, Jack said, 'Do you want them to see us standing here quarrelling?'

Clare gave him an annihilating look, but went to the entry panel and pressed the button for her flat. She looked into the camera and the door buzzed to let her open it. She lived on the third floor. Reluctantly Clare led the way there. Jack had let go his iron grip on her arm but he was close behind, watchful, alert in case she tried to give him the slip.

Jonesy opened the door for her, timing it perfectly as he always did so that she didn't have to ring the bell. Clare took some satisfaction in seeing Jack's eyebrows rise. He'd probably been expecting a young female au pair or a nanny—definitely not a getting-on-for-elderly man in shabby but clean clothes who was giving him a critical once-over.

Clare smiled at Jonesy. 'Everything OK?'

'Perfectly fine, m' dear. Perfectly fine.'

He was still looking at Jack with interest, but Clare didn't introduce them. 'Hang around for a while, will you, please? This—person won't be staying long.'

Jonesy nodded and went into the kitchen.

Leading the way into the sitting-room, Clare shut the door, then turned to Jack. 'All right, so you're here. What do you want?'

Jack looked at her for a moment, sensitive to the antagonism in her voice, in the way she looked at him—even in the way she stood, so slim and defiant. But he hadn't come here to threaten her—and he certainly hadn't come to beg. So, keeping his voice casual, he said, 'Could I have a drink? A whisky, if you have it?'

She hesitated for a moment, not wanting him to stay, not even wanting to offer him any hospitality, but then crossed to a drinks tray resting on a sideboard and poured him a whisky and soda.

She had her back to him, so Jack was able to watch her openly. He remembered that she'd been very thin when they'd made love, her body half-starved from the way she'd been living rough. But she'd been full of a fire and passion so intense that it had amazed him then and he could remember it now. She was still slim, but her figure was rounded in the right places— perhaps because she'd had the child. But was she still as passionate behind the cold face she turned towards him when she handed him the drink?

'You seem to have changed a lot since we first met,' he remarked. 'Now you're very self-assured, independent. I suppose that comes from having to bring up Toby by yourself. I'm sorry that you had to bear all the responsibility alone. If I'd known I would certainly have—'

'Have what?' Clare interrupted tersely. 'Written out a cheque?'

His chin hardening a little, Jack said, 'I would certainly have wanted to help you in any way I could, yes. Financially, or in—'

Clare gave a harsh laugh. 'You seem to forget— you gave me a cheque at the time. So you paid in advance!'

Jack sucked in his breath. So that was it! Vaguely he remembered how upset she'd been when he'd tried to help her. But his father's death had been weighing on his mind. And, yes, he'd felt damned guilty about taking the girl although she'd been willing enough. The classic 'morning after' syndrome. And maybe giving her money had been an attempt to assuage that guilt. But it was amazing to see that she still resented it after all these years. Slowly, feeling his way, he said, 'Is that why you didn't tell me about Toby?'

'Toby is mine. You were—incidental.' Deliberately

she belittled him. Clare wanted him to leave, hating the way she'd been coerced into this conversation and afraid that any moment he would ask to see Toby.

Jack gave a short laugh. Putting down his glass, he went over to where one of Toby's toy trucks lay in a corner. Squatting down, he picked it up, apparently only interested in seeing how it tipped up and the doors opened. But then he glanced up at Clare and his voice was very cold. 'But I do not intend to be just "incidental" any longer.'

With dismay Clare saw that she'd only stiffened his resolve, and suddenly her voice rose in anger as she said hotly, 'If you'd had children of your own, from your marriage, then you wouldn't have cared less about Toby! If I'd told you and you'd given me money then, it would only have been for an abortion! You wouldn't—'

She broke off as Jack straightened and strode to confront her. Standing over her, and suddenly seeming immensely tall and powerful, he said curtly, 'How the hell do you know what I would or wouldn't have done? If I had half a dozen children Toby would still be precious to me. But you have denied me my only son. I've lost the first five years of his life! But I'm not going to let you keep me from him any longer.'

Clare squared up to him, refusing to be intimidated, a lioness protecting her cub. 'You keep away from him. We don't need you. We never have and we never will.' Her voice rose. 'Now get out! Just get out of my home!'

Jack reached out as if to get hold of her and shake her, his jaw thrusting with anger, but the door opened and Jonesy came in. 'You'll wake the boy,' he said reprovingly. 'Do you really want him to hear you quarrelling over him like this?'

Balling his fists, Jack strove to control his rage. 'Who's he?' he demanded.

'The babysitter,' Clare returned shortly.

He stared at her for a moment in disbelief, then turned and strode towards the door. There he turned and said curtly, 'I meant what I said—I intend to be a part of Toby's life, and if I have to fight you to get that, then I'll do whatever it takes.'

Her face white, Clare said, 'Don't you dare threaten me.'

But when he'd gone Clare's legs seemed to lose their strength, and if Jonesy hadn't grabbed her she would have fallen. Trembling, she leaned against his shoulder. 'Oh, God, Jonesy, what am I going to do? He'll take Toby away from me! I know he will.'

Outside on the pavement Jack banged his clenched fist against the wall, furious with himself for having lost his temper, and even more furious with Clare for having goaded him into it. He hadn't meant to threaten her and he'd ended up doing that very thing. Instead of getting access to Toby by negotiation, he would now have to fight for it, with Clare probably pouring poison about him into the boy's ears.

Glancing at his watch, Jack saw that there was more than half an hour before his car was due to return for him. He could have called up the chauffeur on his mobile phone, but instead he decided to take a walk while thinking over his meeting with Clare. His anger made him stride out, and he'd reached the corner when he happened to glance back, just in time to see

the old man Clare had referred to as her babysitter
come out of the flats. Without hesitation, Jack stepped
into a doorway, then followed the man as he headed
in the other direction.

He didn't have to trail him very far; within five
minutes his quarry turned into the entrance of a large,
old Victorian building only a couple of streets away.
Jack gave him time to get inside and then went to
look at the building more closely. At the side of the
door was a notice: HOSTEL FOR HOMELESS MEN. Jack
gasped in astonishment. Good grief! She was using a
drop-out, possibly even a wino, to look after his son!
His jaw hardened with renewed resolve; no way was
he going to allow this to go on. And what he'd just
learned would certainly help his case, he realised with
grim satisfaction. No judge in his right mind would
refuse him access to Toby, or even a say in his upbringing, after this.

CHAPTER FIVE

THE next time Clare saw Jack was on the afternoon of the hearing. She had expected the case to be heard in a courtroom and was surprised when her lawyer led her to a private room where the judge, a woman, merely sat at a large desk. The clerk read out Jack's wish for access to his son. That Clare had expected, but her head came up when she heard that he also wanted a say in his upbringing.

The judge looked at her, not without sympathy, Clare thought, and said, 'Do you admit that Mr Straker is the father of your son?'

For a brief moment Clare hesitated, then said, 'Yes.'

'And does your son know who his father is?'

'I've been forced to tell him. Because of Straker's—notoriety—' she chose the word deliberately '—this case was reported in the press. Some of Toby's schoolfriends got to hear of it and questioned him.'

'You hadn't told him before?'

'No.'

'Why was that?'

Taking her eyes from the judge, Clare let them rest on Jack. 'Because to Straker it was just a one-night stand. Afterwards, he wanted nothing to do with me and told me he was married. He couldn't wait to be

rid of me. I don't want a man like that to have anything to do with my child.'

Jack's eyes narrowed. He nodded at his lawyer,
who stood up and said, 'Do I understand that you
believe Mr Straker will be a corrupting influence on
his son?'

Suspicious, but not sure where he was leading,
Clare said, 'Yes, definitely.'

Smoothly the lawyer said, 'And yet, Miss
Longman, you employ a man who has several times
been arrested for vagrancy and drunkenness to help
look after the boy. I refer to a Mr Albert Jones, at
present residing at a hostel for the homeless. Is that
not so, Miss Longman?'

Clare's face whitened with anger and she threw
Jack a glance of withering contempt. 'I have known
Jonesy—Mr Jones—since Toby was two years old.
He is devoted to him and would never dream of
touching alcohol when he looks after him. In fact he
once saved Toby's life when Toby swallowed part of
a toy and Jonesy got it out of his throat. He is a good,
kind man. I trust him because I know him, and he's
far more trustworthy and reliable than some stranger
from a babysitting agency.

'As for his being homeless, that is no fault of his.
He is an educated and clever man, and he had a really
good job but was made redundant during the reces-
sion. He got another job but was forced to give it up
because his wife became terminally ill, which meant
that he couldn't keep up the mortgage payments on
his house. So he lost his home. And his wife, too,
died.'

As if he hadn't even been listening, the lawyer went

on, 'Yet it is a matter of public record that Mr Jones has twice been arrested for drunkenness within the past three years. And I understand that you are in the habit of making him a present of whisky from time to time.'

'He only ever allows himself to have a binge on his birthday, which is a very sad day for him,' Clare said with dignity. 'And anyone who keeps himself sober the rest of the year for my son's sake deserves the very best malt when he needs it.'

Jack smiled inwardly and found he liked her for that, and for her loyalty. He sympathised with her and with the old man, but this was his strongest weapon and he was going to use it.

The judge intervened. 'Why do you think Mr Straker would be a corrupting influence on your son, Miss Longman?'

'Because he's ruled by money,' Clare answered bluntly. 'It's his god. He tried to buy me off after the—after we were together. I refused it.' Her chin came up. 'I don't sell myself. But he put the cheque in my pocket without me knowing. I was going to tear it up, but then I found I was pregnant so I was forced to use it. I now run my own business, which is successful enough for me not to need any financial help. I can give Toby everything he needs. He has a home, and love and affection. What he doesn't need is some stranger coming into his life and trying to buy his love, to shape him into the sort of son Straker wants.'

She spoke passionately, vehemently, and for a moment Jack felt admiration, perhaps even regret. But there was no way he was going to back down.

Standing up, he said, 'I seem to have been accused of several things here, none of which are true. Yes, I want to be part of my son's life; what father wouldn't want to be? But I want to help, not to corrupt.' He gave a small smile as he said it, as if the whole idea was wholly preposterous.

'OK, I've had some success in my business dealings, so why shouldn't I pass on the rewards of that success for the benefit of my son? The same as every other *father*,' he added, stressing the word, repeating the relationship. 'For the past five years that pleasure, that *right*, has been denied me. I don't want to take over Toby's life, but I would like to share in it. I want to get to know him and for him to get to know me. I appreciate that Miss Longman has done an excellent job so far, but, though he can't be part of a real, complete family, I feel that Toby, too, has the right to know his father.'

The judge looked at Clare. 'That seems a reasonable enough request, Miss Longman.'

Her hands balled into fists so tight that her nails dug into her, Clare answered, 'The fact still remains that Straker made no effort, after he'd kicked me out, to find out if I was OK, that I hadn't become pregnant. He didn't care then. And what happens if he starts showering all this attention and money on Toby but then marries again and has children by his wife? He's still young; it could happen quite easily. And you can bet your life that if he did then he'd just drop Toby, not want to have anything more to do with him. Wouldn't want to waste his money on him,' Clare added with a vengeful glance across the room. 'I refuse to take the risk of letting my son be hurt in that way.'

Immediately Jack was on his feet. His lawyer grabbed his arm, but Jack angrily shook him off. 'That is both insulting and untrue,' he said curtly. 'From the moment I found out that Toby existed I have wanted nothing more than to help him and be part of his life.'

'And do you call bringing this lawsuit helping him?' Clare demanded, forgetting everything else and glaring at Jack.

'I was forced into it by your stubbornness.'

The judge rapped on her desk with a pen and they both turned to look at her, their faces hot and angry. 'I can see that there is very strong feeling in this case. But my sole consideration here is your son.' She paused, and with a shock Clare realised she was speaking to both of them; she had never thought of Toby as being part of them both before. Addressing Jack first, the judge went on, 'Is there any prospect, Mr Straker, of your marrying?'

'No,' Jack answered grimly.

'And you, Miss Longman, do you intend to marry or form a permanent relationship that would give Toby a settled family life?'

Clare hesitated, realising that this was something the judge might take into account and seeing the danger if she said no. So she said cautiously, 'Not—at the moment.'

The judge nodded and said formally, 'I will carefully look into every aspect of this case and I will let you know my decision in due course.' She rose, nodded, and they all filed out.

Clare stopped to speak to her lawyer, who admonished her for losing her cool, making her feel guilty and worried that she'd jeopardised her case. He left her, and she turned to see that Jack, too, had been talking to his lawyer and was about to leave. Running after him, Clare grabbed Jack's arm and spun him round to face her. 'You rat!' she exclaimed. 'How dare you make out that Jonesy is a lush? He's a good, kind man. It wasn't his fault that he lost his job or that his wife died. Only a louse like you would stoop low enough to accuse someone who can't fight back. And did you ever stop to think that Toby might love him? But no, of course you didn't. All you—'

She broke off, her eyes widening in surprise as Jack put a hand over her mouth. 'If you have anything you want to say to me, then you can damn well do it in private. All right?'

Contempt shone in Clare's eyes, but she nodded and Jack took his hand away. 'Scared to have your dirty linen washed in public?' she jeered.

His mouth tightened, but Jack merely said, 'There's a pub not far away; let's go and have a drink.'

Clare hesitated, then shrugged and let him lead her along the street to the pub, where they found a private corner in which to sit.

'What would you like to drink?'

'A glass of dry white wine, please.' She fished some money out of her bag. 'And I'll pay for my own.'

Jack felt like strangling her but he grimly reached out and took the money, carefully giving her a pile of change when he returned with the drinks. Striving to contain his temper, he said, 'I'm glad that we're taking this opportunity to talk.'

'Really?' Clare's tone was sarcastic. 'I thought we only came here because you were afraid of being called a rat in public.'

Gripping his glass, Jack returned evenly, 'Arguing isn't going to help either of us. Why don't we put the question of Toby aside for the moment and just—just talk, get to know each other a little better. Maybe we can find some common ground.'

'You must be joking!'

He turned to look at her and said deliberately, 'Why not? We did once.'

Her colour deepened and Clare lowered her eyes, her long dark lashes brushing her cheeks. 'That was unfair.'

Feeling sudden compassion, Jack said, 'Yes. I'm sorry.'

Her head came up swiftly at that, and she looked at him with something approaching surprised curiosity. Slowly she said, 'I don't feel that I got to know you at all. Not really. Although we were virtually alone for so many days, you showed no interest in me. We never talked.' Some of her fighting spirit asserted itself. 'You never, for example, mentioned that you were married.'

'I was hardly likely to discuss my private life with a complete stranger—someone who'd hidden away in my car,' Jack retorted.

She looked at him, her eyes scathing. 'But, as you said, we weren't—complete strangers, were we?'

He gave a sudden grin. 'Ouch!' He took a drink, then said, 'But I didn't just forget about you. I often wondered how you made out, whether you had found somewhere to live.'

'What a convenient memory you have,' Clare mocked. 'Do you really expect me to believe that?'

Ignoring her, Jack added, 'And I often remember that last night—the night my father died.'

Clare stiffened, thinking that he probably hated her because he'd shown weakness, had let her see how vulnerable he could be. Quickly she said, 'I don't want to discuss the past. The present is the only thing that matters.'

'Perhaps you're right.' Jack looked at her with renewed interest, wondering if she had any sexual hang-ups, whether her experience with him had caused it. The thought disturbed him. He remembered, back at her flat, she'd said that he'd ruined her life; at the time he'd thought she meant because he'd made her pregnant, but now he wondered if it wasn't that simple, whether there was more to it than that.

Her face was averted and he let his eyes run over her. She wasn't beautiful, not in the glamorous model sense that seemed to be the accepted criterion for beauty nowadays, but with her dark hair, pale skin and those expressive eyes she was attractive—even striking. Anyone who'd seen her angry—as she seemed to be all the time with him—would never forget her face, he mused. She had a good figure, too, all that it took to attract men. Jack found himself intrigued as he again remembered their passionate lovemaking.

Feeling his eyes on her, Clare suddenly turned her head and surprised the hunger in his gaze before he could hide it. Her face tightened. 'This is a waste of time. I'm leaving.'

She went to stand up, but he put out a hand to

prevent her. 'No. Don't go. Of course, you're right—
Toby is all that matters. You told the judge he knows
about me; has he—has he asked to meet me?'

'No.'

She said it too fast and he didn't believe her. 'It
seems strange that he has no curiosity about me. Or
have you told him only what you want him to hear?'
His gaze held hers. 'Are you deliberately trying to
turn Toby against me—even before I've had a chance
to meet him?'

Clare gave him one of her most annihilating looks.
'Only someone with a mind like yours would even
think that.'

'I'm glad to hear it. So what did you tell him?'

'That's between me and Toby.'

'I think I have a right to know, Clare.'

She looked away, played with her glass for a few
minutes, then said reluctantly, 'Basically, I just told
him that you were his father. I said that we'd met by
chance, but that you had a home of your own so you
couldn't live with us.' A defiant note coming into her
voice, she added, 'Toby's only five. He doesn't understand. He knows from his friends that sometimes
fathers live with their children and sometimes they
don't. He can accept that. He's happy as he is. I don't
want his life disrupted.'

'I don't want to disrupt it, I want to make his life
fuller.' Jack put his hands under the table before balling them into fists, not wanting her to see how deep
this went. 'I would like to meet Toby,' he said evenly.

'No! You're not going to have any part in his life,
so what's the point?'

'Toby is as much mine as yours, Clare.'

She turned on him at that. 'No, I won't accept that. Just because we—we had sex once and it resulted in a child doesn't mean that Toby is going to want you round him. Do you think he's going to need you, that some basic instinct will take over and he'll love you as a son? Well, he won't. He'll be scared of you, and unsure of himself. You'll make him confused and shy and then you'll get irritable with him which will make him worse. It would be easier for him to meet you as a stranger rather than a potential father. He'll feel threatened. Just as I feel threatened.' She stood up, her voice rising. 'So why don't you just get out of our lives and leave us alone? We don't need you. We never have and we never will!' And, pushing past him, Clare strode out of the pub.

Jack made no attempt to follow her. He bought another drink and sat down moodily. A picture of Clare's face came to his mind—not when she was angry, but as she'd been when he'd first met her at his father's house. She'd looked so young then, and vulnerable, her features sharpened by hunger. Like a child.

Jack felt an intense, deep longing to know what his son looked like. Was there anything of himself in the boy, or was he a replica of his mother? He'd had this longing ever since he'd found out that Toby existed, after that one, amazed glimpse from his car when he had suddenly known with absolute certainty why Clare was so scared, why she had run from him.

Over the weeks the need to see Toby had grown, become an obsession. He yearned to touch him, to feel the warmth of his hand and know that his own blood ran in the boy's veins. But he'd kept this need to see his son under control, had tried to do the right thing by approaching Clare first. And when she wouldn't see him he had gone to get permission from a court. He'd wanted to do it right, but he saw now that Clare would do everything she could to stop him. Suddenly his patience ran out. Tossing down his drink, Jack, too, hurried out of the pub and whistled up a cruising taxi.

Toby's school was a good one, and there was a preponderance of nannies and au pairs waiting to receive their charges. Jonesy, in his shabby, patched clothes, stood out from them like a sore thumb, but they had all got used to him by now and had a friendly greeting for him. Down the street from the entrance Jack sat in the taxi, watching until Jonesy and Toby came out hand in hand, then he paid off the cab and strolled down the road towards them.

They were talking together, Toby excitedly telling Jonesy about a planned school trip to a safari park, when they became aware that a man had stopped in front of them. Jonesy looked up and started in surprise.

He made a gesture as if to ward him off, but Jack said as reassuringly as he could, 'Hello, Jonesy. I think you remember me?'

'Yes, but... Did Clare send you?'

Jack supposed he could have lied, but he shook his head. 'No. I thought I'd just come along and meet you.' He allowed himself to glance down. 'And to meet Toby.'

The boy looked up at him and seemed disconcertingly familiar. For a moment Jack couldn't think why, but then he remembered an old photograph—not of himself, but of his own father as a young boy, probably about the same age as Toby was now. There was the same wide forehead, the straight brows and the good bone structure that made him an attractive child and would one day make him a devilishly handsome young man. Only the eyes were different; Toby looked curiously up at him with eyes that were an exact replica of Clare's. Jack squatted down to Toby's level and smiled at his son. 'Hello, Toby.'

The boy glanced up at Jonesy, who gave a reluctant nod, then said politely, 'Hello. We're all going to a safari park soon.'

'That sounds great. Do you like animals?'

'Yes, but they're not allowed in the flats. I did have a hamster once, but it got out and frightened the cleaning lady half to death. That's what she said—"half to death",' he added with some relish. 'And she said she wouldn't come any more if we kept it, so we took the hamster to school and it lives in the classroom now.'

Jack's lips twitched and he found himself enthralled, his heart already filling with love. He would have liked to take Toby's hand in his, to take him to a place where they could have talked alone, but he knew that was too much to hope for. He was already playing a risky game in coming here at all; he couldn't try for more than this—not yet. So, keeping his voice light, he said, 'Are you any good at drawing? Perhaps you could draw a picture of the hamster for me. What's his name?'

'Cricetus—our teacher said that was the proper name for a hamster, but I used to call him Puffball.'

'I think I like Puffball better,' Jack said gravely.

Toby gave a sudden smile, and Jack saw that it

wasn't only his eyes that he'd inherited from Clare. 'So do I,' Toby said. He looked at Jack with renewed interest. 'Are you a friend of my mummy's?'

'Yes.'

'Like Paul?'

Jack tensed, wondering who 'Paul' was, what relationship he had with Clare, but he said easily, 'No, I don't think so.'

'Definitely not.'

Clare's voice spoke from behind him, and Jack straightened and turned to face her. She was furious, but it was a banked-down rage because of the boy, only showing in her eyes and the tension in her body.

Quietly Jack said, 'You suggested it might be better to meet Toby as a stranger.'

She went to step past him and leaned close as she did so, so that only he could hear when she said, 'Only a rat like you would use that as an excuse.' Turning to Toby, Clare held out her arms. 'Hi, kiddo.'

He gave her a hug, told her about the zoo trip, then took her hand as he looked up at Jack. 'He wants me to do a drawing of Puffball for him.'

'Does he?' Clare glanced at Jack and he held her eyes, his own tense, compelling. She hesitated, trying to fight the force of his will as he stood silently waiting, but then she shot him a look of malevolent hatred before turning to Jonesy. 'I'll walk Toby home, Jonesy. Why don't you come round to the flat in an hour and have some tea with us?'

'All right, m' dear. See you, Toby.'

The old man shambled away and Clare pointed off to the right. 'There's an open space behind the school; why don't we go and sit in there for a few minutes?

Lead the way, Toby.' The boy ran on ahead, and Clare turned to Jack. 'I'll never forgive you for having forced me into this,' she said with venom. 'Never!'

Jack didn't answer. He had no time for Clare's anger. All he could think of was that Toby was finally to know that he was his father, and he was worried about how the boy would react. Clare had assured him that she'd said nothing against him to Toby, but her anger and worry was too strong to be entirely hidden, and children were sensitive to the feelings of those close to them. Toby might have picked up that hatred, and their relationship would be ruined before it started.

There were a few flowerbeds round a piece of lawn, and a blossoming tree with an old wooden seat under it. Swallowing her anger, knowing that this was a moment that Toby would probably remember all his life, Clare put her hand on the back of the seat, gripping it tightly, and managed to smile at her son. 'Toby, do you remember I told you about—about Mr Straker?'

Toby looked at her, his face growing solemn, and nodded. Clare tried, but somehow her voice wouldn't work and she was unable to go on. After a moment Toby turned large eyes on Jack. 'Are you—are you Mr Straker?' he asked nervously.

'Yes.' Jack found that his voice had grown husky. 'I'm your father, Toby.'

Toby immediately went to Clare, pressing himself against her legs and searching for her hand. 'He just came to meet you,' Clare said quickly, reassuringly. 'He just wanted to say hello. He won't be coming home with us. *Definitely* not.'

Perhaps the panic sounded in her voice, because Toby dragged his eyes from Jack to look up at her. He put his other hand on hers and squeezed it, almost as if he was doing the comforting. He looked again at Jack, and must have been reassured by what he saw because he said, 'I'll do a drawing of Puffball for you, if you like.'

'Thank you. I'd like that very much.'

'Have you got another boy?' Toby asked.

'No, nor a girl. Only you, son.' He said the last word tentatively, almost as if he was afraid to use it, but in his own ears it sounded the best word Jack had ever uttered.

Clare tensed, hating him for it. She felt coerced, manipulated, cheated, her stable, contented life ruined. She felt fiercely protective for Toby, and would have given anything for Jack not to have found out about him. But he had. And now, for Toby's sake, she had to pretend that nothing was the matter— which was the hardest part of all. 'We'd better be getting home.'

'Can we have a look at the car in the shop on the way?' Toby asked.

'OK, but only for five minutes.'

They left the garden but Jack fell into step beside them, with Toby in the middle.

'Don't let us keep you. I'm sure you have lots of important things to do—starting a few companies, taking over existing ones, making another million, that kind of thing,' Clare said acidly.

'I've already done my quota for the day,' Jack returned equably. 'So I might as well walk you home.'

'Thanks, but we're quite capable of walking home

alone.' The expressive look Clare threw him over Toby's head said far more than that. The message came across clear as day: go away, get out of our lives!

But Jack ignored it, and was still with them when they reached a shop selling all kinds of second-hand goods from old pots and pans to collector's items. Toby pushed open the door and dived inside. 'Can I see it, please?' he asked breathlessly.

The plump, middle-aged woman minding the shop laughed at him. 'It isn't any different from last time.' She reached to a shelf behind her and brought out a box which she put on the counter. Toby climbed onto a chair so that he could see better, and reverently opened the box. Inside was a model of a silver-grey car. Shyly Toby looked at Jack and said, 'It's James Bond's car. From the films. It's an *original* model.'

'Really?' Jack leaned on the counter to examine it more closely. 'Does the number plate turn round?'

'Yes. And look.' Toby excitedly displayed all the car's gadgets, touching it delicately. 'It costs a lot of money, but Mrs Osmond is keeping it for me until I have enough.' He fished in his pocket and brought out a fifty-pence coin. It was duly entered in a little book and the car put away.

Jack felt an overwhelming urge to pay for the car and give it to him, to see the boy's face light up when he knew it was his, now. He caught Clare's eyes on him, knew that she was expecting him to do just that, and easily resisted the temptation. He began to talk to Toby about cars and was astonished at the boy's knowledge.

'I've got a lot at home,' Toby told him.

'Perhaps you'd show them to me one day.' Jack knew that the remark was inviting fire from Clare, but it evidently pleased Toby.

'OK.'

They walked along towards the flat, and Jack felt a small hand shyly take hold of his. He glanced down at Toby's upturned face and his heart filled to over-flowing. It was the best moment of his life, and he had to turn his head away so that no one would see the idiotic tears of happiness that came to his eyes.

CHAPTER SIX

TOBY was safely in bed at last, bathed, a story read to him and fast asleep. Leaving Clare free to pace the floor of the sitting-room and pour out the story of everything that had happened that day to Paul Venton's willing ears.

He sat on the sofa, drink in hand, and thought how fantastic she looked. So far their relationship had been a platonic one, the two of them having been originally drawn together by their mutual love of antiques, and this had grown into an easy friendship. But no more than that. The fact that she was confiding in him now made Paul wonder if their friendship had reached a new stage.

'I couldn't agree with you more,' he said when she'd told him just what she thought of Straker. 'But then I'm biased. I already have reason to dislike him intensely.'

'You do?' Clare was immediately intrigued and came to sit beside him. 'Why?'

'Didn't you know? He's in the same sort of business that I'm in. We're often competitors.' His mouth twisted wryly. 'Unfortunately there have been several occasions when Straker has managed to do a deal and take a lucrative contract from right under our noses. So I have no reason to like him, either. The man seems to live up to his nickname; he certainly has a charmed touch,' he added with asperity.

He was right, Clare thought; Jack certainly seemed to have a charmed touch where Toby was concerned. She'd never seen him accept a stranger so easily, and the way he'd taken Jack's hand hadn't been lost on her. It had hurt, seeing that, filling her heart with a great, engulfing feeling of intense jealousy. She'd wanted to snap at Toby to let go, but she'd known she couldn't; it would have been grossly unfair to take it out on Toby. It wasn't the child's fault; he probably thought that was what he was supposed to do with a father. He had been overly excited tonight—asking about Jack, wanting to know if they would see him again. Clare had finally said curtly that she didn't know and Toby had become quiet, aware of her anger.

Clare was annoyed with herself about that, but she'd just about had enough today. 'I'm really worried about all this,' she admitted to Paul.

'Try to put it out of your mind until you get the result of the hearing. And don't forget—Straker having forced himself on the boy like that could be to your advantage. The judge might well hold that against him. I should tell your lawyer about it and make sure that the judge knows.'

'I already have; I phoned his office earlier.' Clare smiled suddenly. 'Poor Paul; I'm crying out all my troubles on your shoulders. You must be bored out of your mind.'

'Don't be silly. I only wish I could help in some way.'

The doorbell rang and Clare went to let Jonesy in. Then she and Paul left to go out to dinner. They went out together on a fairly frequent but irregular basis, although she seemed to have seen more of him recently.

Paul was quite a lot older than Clare, almost twenty years older, and they were happy to act as escort to each other when one was needed, or to have dinner together at some gourmet place that Paul had found and wanted to try, as tonight. Clare enjoyed her evenings with Paul, but had no intention of letting the friendship become at all intimate. She had no wish to have a serious or really close relationship with any man, and if she did it certainly wouldn't be with Paul. He was nice, he was good company, and he knew how to look after a woman, but he was a different generation, and sometimes she found him a bit stuffy. She was still young and there were times when she wanted to party, to let her hair down at a disco and dance the night away.

As a teenager she'd been wild, a rebel against the petty tyranny of the great-aunt and uncle who had reluctantly brought her up after her grandmother had died, and who had tried to force their dated standards and monotonous lifestyle on her. Having Toby and building up her business had taken a great deal of the wildness out of her, but there were still times when she longed to break loose, to rebel against all her responsibilities for a while and run a little wild.

But with Paul that was impossible; he was far too conscious of his image ever to let his hair down in public—or in private, either, Clare guessed. Which was why she could never see herself getting serious about him—and why she enjoyed going out with him. There was never any hassle, he didn't try to push her into a closer relationship that she didn't want. Perhaps he guessed that if he did she would just walk away, as she had with other men who'd tried to get too close.

The following day Clare had lunch with Tanya, the old schoolfriend she'd seen at the charity auction. They hadn't met up for some time so there was quite a lot to catch up on. Clare expected to be bombarded with questions about Jack, and although she did start off by asking about him it soon turned out that Tanya had troubles of her own and was looking for a sympathetic ear to pour them into.

'I was amazed to read about you and Jack Straker of all people,' Tanya began. 'I often wondered who Toby's father was. How long did the affair last?'

'It was very brief,' Clare said tersely. 'How's Brian?'

'Oh, OK, I suppose.' Tanya dismissed her husband. 'Was he good in bed?'

'It was so long ago, I've forgotten.'

Tanya grinned. 'I bet you haven't. I bet he was great; he certainly looks as if he'd be great. All those muscles. I wonder if he treats his women rough. They say that men from working-class backgrounds are often far more fun in bed. Is it true?'

'I told you; I can't remember,' Clare said repressively.

'Liar.' Tanya's face grew wistful. 'You are lucky to be free to sleep around. You get a really guilty conscience if you even think about it when you're married.'

'Which means, I take it, that you have been thinking about it?'

'Well... Rather more than thinking, actually.'

Clare's eyebrows rose. 'You mean you have a lover?'

Tanya sighed. 'At the moment I'm holding out.'

'You mean playing hard to get?'

'No! I'm pretty serious about this man. It isn't a casual thing; we've really fallen for each other and he's talking marriage.' She leaned closer. 'The trouble is that Brian's got wind of it and I've a severe case of GBS on my hands.'

'"GBS"? What on earth's that?'

'Oh, of course, you're not married, so you wouldn't know. It's "Glacial Bed Syndrome". No warmth, turning your back on your wife, sulks—all that hurt-little-boy routine.'

Clare couldn't help laughing. 'Tanya, that sounds dreadful! Do married people really behave like that?'

'Married *men* do. I'm supposed to beg and plead for forgiveness and promise him my undying love if only he'll be nice to me again. But I happen to know that Brian went away to a so-called conference with a woman who wasn't his PA, so he can turn into a lump of solid ice for all I care.'

'So are you sure this affair you're having isn't just revenge?' Clare asked. 'It would be a bit fatal to get a divorce, marry this man and find that you're still in love with Brian, now, wouldn't it?'

'Of course; and Brian is the father of my children and all that. I do want to be sure, and I'd really like to get to know this new man better before I take any irreversible step, but it's difficult for me to meet him without Brian—or anyone else—finding out. It would be terrible if it appeared in a gossip column, for instance. It's OK for you, of course, but—'

'It is not OK for me,' Clare snapped. 'That damn man is taking me to court to get access to Toby.'

'Well, if Jack Straker is his father I wonder you don't welcome him with open arms. He's supposed to be phenomenally wealthy. Think what he could do for Toby.'

Realising that Tanya's principles were a million light years away from her own, Clare said, 'What are you going to do about your lover?'

'Well...' Her friend gave her an assessing look. 'Actually, I wondered if you'd let us borrow your flat.' She saw Clare's mouth fall open and added hastily, 'It would just be so that we could talk. It's so difficult to find somewhere really private. And you living in a block of flats, no one would know that we were going to the same place. I could say I was visiting you for lunch, or something, and my—my friend could be visiting just anyone who lived there. So it would be perfect, you see. Please say yes, Clare. I'm at my wits' end. And you know I'd do the same for you.'

'I don't anticipate being in a position where I need to lie,' Clare said shortly. Then laughed at herself. 'God, that was so pompous. Who is this man, Tanya?'

'I can't tell you; I promised I wouldn't.'

'Is he married?'

'Sort of.'

'How can you be "sort of" married?'

'You'd be surprised. I think most of the people I know are only sort of married nowadays. Will you lend us the flat? It will only be for a month or so, until I make up my mind. And it will only be to *talk*.'

Clare didn't quite believe that, and she didn't want to help break up a marriage, but Tanya was one of her few close friends. Even so, she would have said no if she hadn't felt that Tanya was really motivated by revenge and that in the end would probably stay with her husband once she got this new man out of her system. So Clare reluctantly nodded. 'I'll have a couple of spare keys cut for you. But be sure to phone me first, OK?'

She was overwhelmed with thanks, but had second, third and fourth thoughts about it almost at once. Clare didn't like the thought of her home being used for secret assignations, and she was rather worried about what Brian might do if he ever found out. But she had given her consent, so there was no going back.

Her main worry at the moment was Toby. He had done the drawing of Puffball for Jack, taking great pains over it and carefully writing his name at the bottom. They had found a very large envelope for it and had sent it off nearly a week ago, but there had been no response from Jack. When the phone rang or the post came Toby would look at her expectantly, and Clare's heart filled with angry bitterness when she saw the disappointment in his eyes when she shook her head.

So this was Jack's idea of fatherhood, she thought furiously. To encourage the boy and then leave him flat. After all the protestations he'd made at the court about wanting to be a part of Toby's life, too. Clare was scarcely able to contain her anger; she decided to give him just a couple more days and then to inform her lawyer.

But it was early on the following evening, a Saturday, when the doorbell rang and Toby, running to look at the viewer, said excitedly, 'It's him.'

'Who?' Clare called from the kitchen.

Toby hesitated, then said, 'Mr Straker.'

Clare wiped her hands and came to the screen. Jack was looking up at the camera, one eyebrow raised as he waited. Clare picked up the door phone and saw Jack do the same. 'What do you want?'

'I've called to see Toby.'

'You have no right to do that.'

'I want to thank him for the drawing.'

'You could have telephoned him, or written— you've had plenty of time.'

'I've been away,' Jack said evenly. 'I'd like to explain that to him.'

Clare glanced at Toby. He couldn't hear what was being said, but he was watching her with large, expectant eyes. Clare's heart misgave her, but she couldn't let Toby down. 'You can come up,' she said reluctantly. 'But only for ten minutes.' And she pressed the front-door release.

Jack must have been somewhere hot; his skin was a couple of shades darker than when they'd last seen him. Toby opened the door to him, but Jack was almost hidden behind a gorgeous daisy bush in a large earthenware pot. 'Hello, Toby.' He looked at Clare and nodded. 'Thanks for letting me come up.' He looked round. 'Where would you like it?'

'What makes you think I want a present from you?'

Jack looked at her and his eyes crinkled with

amusement. 'Who says it's for you?' He set the pot down on a small table where, Clare had to admit, it certainly enhanced the room. If he had brought roses, or orchids, or something equally expensive and exotic, Clare could easily have thrown them back at him, but the daisy bush was so lovely, the dozens of white heads so delicate, that she immediately fell in love with it.

'Thanks for the drawing, Toby. I like it very much.' Jack glanced at Clare, but as she didn't look as if she was going to ask him to sit down he sat down anyway, choosing a low armchair.

Toby came over and leaned on the arm. 'Mummy said you would phone, but you didn't.'

'No, sorry about that, Toby, but I've been away. I only got back today, so I thought I'd come straight over and tell you how much I like it.' Jack didn't add that he had been in South Africa on business, and had rung his secretary, who'd mentioned the large envelope that had arrived for him. He'd told him to open it, and when he'd heard what it contained had immediately decided to take a break in negotiations and fly home. Now he was infinitely glad that he had; there was uncertainty in Toby's voice, and Jack didn't ever want Toby to be uncertain about him.

Jack asked him about the drawing and soon had Toby chatting happily to him. It wasn't till then that he reached into his pocket and brought out a flat parcel. 'I thought you might have used up a lot of your colouring pencils doing the drawing for me, so I brought you some more,' Jack explained.

Toby looked at the parcel then glanced at Clare, who was standing in the doorway, leaning against the jamb, watching them. Clare had little choice but to nod, and Toby said a polite, 'Thank you very much,' before unwrapping the parcel. Inside was a box of pencils—nothing too elaborate, but he smiled with genuine pleasure.

'I thought you might like to do a drawing of the flowers,' Jack suggested.

'Shall I do it now?'

'That would be great.'

Toby settled himself at the table and Clare went into the kitchen. After a couple of minutes Jack followed her. She turned on him and, keeping her voice down to a low, venomous snare, said, 'You are a cunning, conniving—'

'Rat. I know.'

'I was about to use a much stronger word. This is the second time you've forced your way into my home and—'

'Hardly forced,' Jack protested.

'OK—conned, then. And I don't like it. You know you're not welcome here.'

'Do I?' Jack let his eyes run over her. Tonight Clare looked far more like the young girl he had known six years ago. Her hair was loose, her face unmade-up and she wore jeans and a casual shirt under a sweater. Seeing her like that made him remember the one night they'd spent together, and he suddenly wished that she didn't hate him so much. The thought was disturbing and Jack pushed it out of his mind, instead saying, 'No date with Paul tonight?'

Clare was immediately suspicious. 'Paul?'

'Toby mentioned that you were seeing someone of that name,' Jack explained.

'So what's it to you? Who I see or what I do are no business of yours.'

'Except in so far as you're the mother of my child,' Jack said evenly.

Clare gave an astonished, angry laugh. 'Oh, I see. So you're threatening me now. Trying to make out that I'm an unfit mother or something?'

'Not at all,' Jack said quickly, cursing his mistake. 'It's just that—'

But he had no time to explain as Clare said acidly, 'How dare you? You're the one who has a failed marriage behind him. You're the one who cheated on his wife, who committed adultery—not me. How many times did you do that, Straker? How many women did you have on the side before your wife threw you out?' she jeered.

Jack's face had tightened. 'That is not why we split up. And it's none of your damn business anyway.'

'Neither is it your business who I choose to go out with. Someone with a reputation like yours oughtn't to be allowed anywhere near Toby. So don't you ever, *ever* accuse me of being an unfit mother. Do you hear me?'

'Yes.' She was a lioness again, he saw, ready to spit and scratch and fight to protect her cub. And because Toby was his cub, too, Jack held up a placating hand. 'I really didn't mean to imply anything of the sort. I just meant that anything that affects Toby must therefore be of interest to me.' He sighed as Clare's chin came up, and he realised that last remark hadn't been very tactful either. He gave a rueful laugh and put up a hand to push his hair off his forehead. 'I'm only digging myself deeper into the mire, aren't I?'

He tried to sound reasonable. 'Do we have to be enemies, Clare?'

'Yes!'

'I don't want to take Toby away from you, you know.'

'That's what you say now, but if you gain access to him then you'll try to undermine me. You'll want him sent away to school, you'll take him on holidays, try to win him over with expensive presents. Do you think I don't know what you're trying to pull?'

'You've got it wrong,' Jack said exasperatedly. 'What do I have to do to convince you?'

'Just walk out of the door and never come back.'

She meant it; she really meant it. Slowly Jack shook his head. 'I'm afraid you don't know me very well, Clare. If I want something then I go all out to get it. I don't give up. And right now there is nothing in the world I want more than to be a father to Toby.'

Clare recognised his indomitability and her face whitened. But she should have known; how else would he have succeeded so well in business if he hadn't got this streak of determined ruthlessness? But she didn't feel defeated by it. She had learnt to be good in business herself and there was no way she was going to let Jack browbeat her. 'You've had your ten minutes,' she said abruptly. 'Now get out, Straker.'

Jack's hands tightened into fists that he shoved in his pockets. It was a long time since anyone had dared to speak to him so rudely, and even longer since anyone had ordered him around. But, his anger under control, he said, 'My name is Jack.'

'Is it? I've never had occasion to use it.'

His eyes widened at that, and he sent his mind winging swiftly back in time. It was true, he thought, that when they'd been together all those years ago if she'd addressed him at all it had been as Mr Straker. But then another memory came back, sharp and clear. When they'd been sitting on her bed together Clare had put her arms round him to comfort him, had stroked his face on which the tears of grief had still been wet, and had said softly, 'Poor Jack. Poor Jack.' And later, when they were making love, she had gasped out his name—not once, but over and over again, as she had reached the dizzying peak of passion and ecstasy.

The memory of that moment, and of his own shared delight, must have shown in his eyes. Clare gave a small gasp and put out a hand as if to ward him off, although he made no attempt to touch her. 'Don't,' she pleaded huskily.

But Jack's face was still sharp, his eyes heavy with remembered passion as he said thickly, 'You did once; you used my name once.'

Clare took a step away from him, came up against the sink and put her hands behind her to grip its edge. 'Get out of here,' she managed.

Standing like that threw her breasts forward, filling the sweater, and it made Jack want to reach out and touch them, fondle them. He wanted to see her as she'd been then—naked and eager, crying out his name in passion. He felt his body start to harden, so fierce was the sudden need. Abruptly he turned away, so that she wouldn't see and recognise his lust. For what else could it possibly be? He could imagine Clare's scorn, her derision, how she would denigrate his virility. Again he reached up to push back his hair, but his hand was unsteady now. Trying desperately to take his mind off her, he said as he reached the door, 'We should be hearing the court's decision any day now. Will you abide by it?'

'Will you, when it's in my favour?' she countered. There was a small frown between her eyes as she watched him. For a moment there... But he seemed perfectly in control now, so maybe she had been wrong.

'I'll be given access, Clare; I'm sure of it.'

'If you are, then I'll appeal.'

He gave a grim smile. 'That's what I thought. You'll be wasting your time.'

'Maybe not—when I tell them how you've already forced yourself on Toby.'

Jack gave an impatient gesture, went to speak, but just then the door opened and Toby came in. 'I haven't finished the drawing yet,' he told Jack. Then he turned to Clare. 'Is dinner nearly ready? I'm hungry.'

'Oh, heavens!' Clare had forgotten all about dinner. 'Sorry, honey, it won't take long.'

'Can Mr Straker—' Toby stopped, looking uncertain but pleading. 'Can my daddy stay?'

It was a very small, ordinary kind of word for a child to use, but it was the first time Toby had ever used it. In Clare it caused consternation, and in Jack a surge of triumph. He saw that she was going to refuse, so said very quickly, 'That's very nice of you, Toby. I'd very much like to stay. That's if your mother doesn't mind, of course.' And the look he gave Clare was an open challenge.

But she wasn't about to be coerced any longer, and said, 'Unfortunately there isn't enough for three.'

'Perhaps a take-away, then? Or shall we all go out somewhere? What's your favourite place, Toby?'

'It's much too late to go out,' Clare said sharply. 'Toby is always in bed by eight, latest.'

'We could have a pizza,' Toby piped up.

'No, it's impossible. I—' Clare broke off. Toby was looking up at her with puzzled, unhappy eyes. He was so young, how could he possibly understand the tension that lay between them? Perhaps he might never understand that what had happened between her and Jack had raised an insuperable, unbridgeable barrier— and Toby himself, instead of being something in common, had only served to push them forever apart. But, right now, all Toby knew was that his father had come to see him and he wanted him to stay. For him it was that simple. Clare wanted to shout and scream at Jack to get out, but she had to bite her lip and say, 'OK, we'll have a pizza.' She looked at Jack with naked hatred in her eyes. 'But Toby goes to bed at eight.'

He nodded. 'Thanks.' And because it would be stupid to quarrel with her, added, 'I won't stay too long.'

'You already have,' she said tartly.

Jack could afford to give a rueful smile at that. He knew he was winning with Toby, and he felt exultant. The two of them had quite a discussion over the choice of pizzas, then went off to phone through the order, and down to the entrance together to collect them when they finally arrived.

Clare had set three places at the table by the window that overlooked the gardens and they sat down to eat. For Clare it brought back recollections of when she and Jack had eaten together at his father's house—meals that she had cooked for him. They hadn't talked much then, and she didn't want to talk now, but she remembered that she'd been grateful to Jack for letting her stay, for not giving her hell for having hidden in his car.

It all seemed so long ago, that time, almost as if it had happened to a different person. Maybe she *was* a different person. She certainly felt light years away from the insecure teenager who had run away to London. And it had definitely taught her not to give herself so easily—and to a virtual stranger. Although it was odd, really, she reflected. That night she'd thought she had known Jack through and through, had reached to the core of his being. Which just showed how wrong you could be.

Toby was chatting to Jack, still a little shy at times but rapidly becoming confident with him. And Jack was delighting in their conversation, learning to adjust mentally to Toby's level of understanding without talking down to him. From time to time he glanced at Clare, but she sat in withdrawn silence. At first he thought she was sulking—which would, he supposed, be understandable—but then he decided that she was lost in her own thoughts. He could guess what they were! His face became a little grim; she was probably composing the letter she was going to write to her lawyer about his 'forcing his way into her home.'

But it was worth it to sit here like this with Toby. It seemed so right. But Jack couldn't help wondering what it would have been like if he'd had children by his wife—then immediately he was glad he hadn't. The divorce had been messy enough as it was, without children to complicate things. And he definitely couldn't see his ex-wife as a mother. Not like Clare, who was ready to fight him for her son.

She and Toby were good together; anyone could see that. But Toby's eager acceptance of him showed that he was old enough for a father figure to have an important place in his life. But once again Jack wondered who Paul was, and just where he fitted into things. Toby didn't seem to mention him much; Jonesy's was the name he used most often.

Turning to Clare, Jack said, 'How did you come to meet Jonesy?'

She was immediately on the defensive. 'Trying to dig up more dirt on him?'

'I'm interested, that's all.'

'He saved my life,' Toby put in.

Jack remembered Clare saying something like that at the hearing. 'Then I'm very grateful to him. How did it happen?' he asked Clare.

She hesitated for a moment, then shrugged and said, 'It was about three years ago; we'd gone to the park to feed the squirrels. A piece of a new toy I'd just bought for Toby came off in his mouth and it got stuck in his throat. Luckily Jonesy was sitting on a park bench and ran over and saved him. So we brought Jonesy home for a meal and a bath, and I managed to find him a place at the hostel. Since then he's always looked after Toby for me when I've needed someone.'

'I was surprised when I talked to him,' Jack said carefully. 'He seems too well-educated to be a drop-out.'

'It wasn't from choice. He had a good job, a large

house on a mortgage, a loving wife. Everything was fine for him, but then his company was taken over and he was made redundant.' Clare shot Jack a glance. 'You should know all about that!' She waited, but Jack didn't rise to the bait, so she went on, 'Jonesy managed to find another job, but then his wife became ill and he had to give it up to look after her. He couldn't keep up the payments on the house and it was repossessed. He had to take his sick wife from the home she'd loved and move into a one-bedroomed flat. That really hurt him, because he felt that he'd failed her. When she finally died he went to pieces. He'd never drunk before in his life, but it was the only comfort he could find. When we found him he'd been living rough for several years, but now he hardly drinks at all—and never near Toby.'

'Yes, I remember.' Jack looked at her with new respect. Even though the old man had saved the boy's life, it still took someone special not just to have paid him off but to have taken Jonesy into their home and made him almost part of the family. The family; Jack liked the sound of that. His own mother had died before he'd really known her, and he and his father had never been close—that was one of the reasons why he was so determined to be a real father to Toby. But he wished now that he hadn't used Jonesy as a possible means to that end.

He went to say as much, but Clare turned away. 'Time to get ready for bed, Toby.'

The boy went off obediently, and Jack, brainwashed by a thousand films and television programmes, said, 'Don't you have to help him? Bath him, read him a story, that kind of thing?'

'He's five. He can get himself ready,' she said lightly. Usually she did help, of course, but she knew that if she did so tonight Jack would want to at least watch, even if not be a part of it, and she found that she couldn't bear that. It was their routine, hers and Toby's, and as such was precious to her. No way would she willingly share it with this man who was determined to push his way into their lives.

Clare didn't feel at ease alone in the room with him, so got up to clear the table. To her surprise, Jack began to help, following her into the kitchen with a load of dishes. It annoyed Clare because she'd wanted to be alone to think, so she said waspishly, 'My, my! Did your wife train you to be so domesticated?'

His eyes flicked at her and he frowned. 'I live alone. I'm used to clearing up after myself.'

'Really?' It was stupid but she couldn't stop. 'You don't even have anyone to cook or clean for you? You just tie your frilly pinny round your waist and run around with the vacuum cleaner, do you? Flick a duster over the furniture and—'

Jack grabbed her wrist and swung her round to face him, making her drop the cutlery she was holding. It fell with a noisy clatter as she looked into Jack's angry eyes. 'I know you don't want me here,' he said curtly. 'You've made that plain enough. But do you have to behave like an ostrich with its head stuck in the sand? We need to approach this in an adult and civilised way so that—'

'So that you can get what you want,' Clare cut in. 'Well, hell, no! I'm going to behave exactly as I please in my own home, and I am *not* going to let you walk all over me. You may be able to charm a child like Toby but to me you're as clear as a window-pane—I can see right through you. And I don't like what I see.'

'You liked me well enough once,' Jack pointed out grimly.

'On the contrary; I merely felt sorry for you.'

'Did you?' Jack's hand tightened on her wrist. 'And do you make a habit of sleeping with every man you feel sorry for?'

Her free hand came up to hit him. Jack saw it coming and prepared to ward off the slap, but, unlike any woman he'd known before, Clare bunched her fist and aimed a full-blown punch. He ducked out of the way, and the force of it brought her off-balance so that she fell against him. Jack caught her and put his arms round her, holding hers clamped to her sides so that she couldn't try to hit him again. She tossed her head angrily, and Jack realised she must have recently washed her hair; the clean scent of it filled his senses.

'Let go of me,' she said furiously, the hatred back in the eyes that flashed fire at him.

'I'm not sure I dare. You pack quite a punch.'

'You chauvinist! Don't you dare condescend to me! God, I hate men who try to dominate women by sheer physical strength.'

Jack laughed, suddenly enjoying himself. To tease her a little, perhaps even to teach her a lesson, he bent her back against his arm, letting her feel his power over her. It brought her body, curved in all the right places, up against the length of his. He expected her to start yelling at him in a fury, to struggle to get free. What he didn't expect was the sudden panic in her face. For a moment he didn't understand, but then he realised she was afraid he was going to kiss her. It hadn't been his intention, but now he wanted to, had a great urge to take her lips and use sensuality to overcome her resistance, to make her surrender to his will.

It was only a fleeting temptation before common sense reasserted itself, but Clare had read the intention in his eyes and said tightly, 'Don't you dare!'

It was the wrong thing to say. Jack had refused few challenges in his life, and this wasn't going to be one of them. His arm tightened and he drew her towards him, slowly and deliberately, letting her feel her helplessness against his strength. His spare hand he put in her hair, holding her head so that she couldn't turn away. She didn't close her eyes but glared murderously up at him, her mouth clamped tight shut. It was a while since he'd had a woman, and the feel of her in his arms, of her body taut against his own, excited him all over again. Clare was resisting him now, holding herself rigid, exerting all her strength to keep her head from his, but Jack drew her ever closer until their lips were just an inch apart. Then he lightly brushed her lips with his—and let her go.

Clare stumbled backwards, caught off-balance by the suddenness of it. She stared at him, mentally off-balance, too. 'Why did you stop?' she demanded, her voice unsteady.

'Didn't you want me to?'

'I didn't want you to start! It was your over-worked ego that needed to prove the "I'm a big, strong man and you're only a feeble little woman" bit.'

'Is that so? Well, maybe we proved something else

as well—that you're not fighting just to keep Toby away from me, Clare. You're fighting yourself!'

She gave a laugh of derision. 'That's ridiculous.'

'Think about it. Think about the way you denied that I was Toby's father. Think how you keep denying you felt anything that night. You were there. You were part of it,' he said brutally. 'Toby's was no immaculate conception.' He held her eyes. 'And you're fighting the fact that you're not immune to me now.'

A bright flush coloured her cheeks. 'You bastard! Get out. Get out!'

'Don't worry, I'm going.' But at the door Jack turned and said tersely. 'Say goodnight to *our* son for me.'

When he got back to his flat Jack picked up a folder of work, but felt strangely restless and started pacing the floor—a thing he seemed to have been doing quite a bit lately. It wasn't just anger over Clare. He realised he was woman-hungry. It was still early yet; there was time to call someone, take her out to a club and maybe—probably—end up spending the night.

Jack reached for the phone, looked up a number and began to dial it. But then stopped. The memory of Clare's taut body held close against his suddenly filled his mind. It should have made him feel even more randy, but instead it gave him a surprising revulsion for the night he'd planned. It was too contrived, the sex too obviously premeditated. Sex would satisfy his body, but he knew it wouldn't be enough.

Slowly he replaced the receiver, realising that his sense of frustration was as much in his mind, perhaps even in his heart, as in his body.

Clare hardly slept that night. She had written out an acerbic account of Jack's behaviour which she intended to take round to the court and hand to the judge first thing Monday morning. But when the mail clattered through the letter-box as they were having breakfast that day she found that she was too late. The court had already awarded Jack access.

CHAPTER SEVEN

'IT ISN'T full access,' Clare told Paul over champagne and smoked salmon sandwiches during the interval of the performance at The Royal Opera House the following evening. 'I suppose I ought to be pleased about that, but I'd much rather he had been refused.'

'You're going to appeal, of course?'

'Oh, yes. But that could take ages, and in the meantime Toby is getting used to seeing Straker.'

'What exactly were the terms?'

'He's allowed to see Toby for one morning or afternoon a week, and I can be there if I like—which I most certainly do. Heaven knows where he might take Toby if they were alone. The position is to be reviewed after six months, unless my circumstances change, when it will be reviewed at once. My lawyer explained they put that clause in because I might get married, in which case Toby would—in their eyes—have a conventional, settled home and wouldn't need a father figure so much.'

She gave an angry sigh. 'It makes me so mad. We were perfectly happy, the two of us, until this happened. Now some bureaucrat thinks Toby is a deprived child just because there isn't a man permanently in his life.'

'And are you likely—to get married?'

Clare shook her head with an impatient gesture. 'No, of course not.'

'Why so certain?' Paul let his eyes rest on her with pleasure. She was looking particularly striking to-night, in a deep green velvet dress with long sleeves and a straight skirt that did wonders both for her fig-ure and her face, the colour emphasising her good bone structure and bringing out the green in her hazel eyes. But then she always looked good. It was a pleas-ure to be seen out with her; he revelled in the envious glances he got from other men, and her wit and vi-vacity always enlivened the evening.

'I'm OK as I am.' Clare smiled a little. 'And, any-way, I have a very busy lifestyle; I don't think I could fit anything else into my schedule.'

'I hardly think a husband would want to be part of a timetable, to be fitted in when you can spare the time,' Paul pointed out.

'Of course not—which is why I don't want one.' She smiled at him. 'All I need is someone like you, who's willing to share a pleasant evening together oc-casionally.'

Seeing her smile, Paul thought that he would like to share much more than that; but he had no illusions; he knew that if he started to get serious he would lose her, because she wasn't in love with him. She liked him, enjoyed his company, but she had let him know right from the start that that was as far as it went. If he suggested an affair she would probably be mildly amused. If he suggested marriage she would definitely laugh at him. Unless... A thought occurred to him, and Paul sat pensively through the second half of the opera as the idea continued to hold his mind.

He said nothing about it to Clare, however, and she had to face up to seeing Jack again when he came to spend a morning with Toby. It had been decided that Saturday mornings would be the best time for them all, and he had rung to suggest going out somewhere, to which Clare had agreed because she didn't want him at the flat again. She expected they'd go to the zoo, or somewhere similar, but Jack sent his chauffeur to pick them up and drive them down to the river Thames, and he dropped them off near the Tower of London where Jack was waiting.

He was wearing casual clothes—jeans and a sweater—reminding Clare of the way he'd looked when she'd first known him. Clare put that out of her mind, instead concentrating on how much she hated him, especially after the arrogant way he'd behaved the last time she'd seen him. She expected him to flaunt his triumph at getting custody in her face, and was all ready to be really cutting in return, but his smile of welcome included her as well as Toby.

'Are we going round the Tower?' she asked, knowing that Toby had already been there.

'No.' Jack gestured towards the river. 'We're going to the bridge.'

And go over Tower Bridge they did, taking the lift to the walkway high over the river and then going down underground to where all the machinery that had once been used to raise and lower the bridge for passing shipping was housed. It was defunct now, of course, the mechanism had changed to electric power years ago, but Jack seemed to know all about how the machines had worked and he carefully explained it all to Toby, being very patient with him and answering his dozens of questions.

Standing a little apart, Clare watched them. It

wasn't the kind of place that she would have thought to take Toby, and she would never have held his attention like this because she didn't know the first thing about engineering. It was easy to see that the boy was fascinated by the huge machines—and fascinated by Jack, too. Toby allowed Jack to pick him up to get a better view, and put a tentative arm round Jack's neck. Feeling it, Jack turned his head and smiled at Toby.

Clare didn't think she would ever forget that moment, the way they looked then: the two faces, so different and yet so alike, smiling at each other, taking that first step to the male mystery of bonding that shut women out. And it was in that instant that Clare knew that Toby would never again be hers alone. He had given some of his heart and love to Jack, and her own relationship with him would never be the complete centre of his life as it had been before.

A great, cold rage filled her, swamping all other emotions. There was no way Jack deserved the love of her innocent son. He was completely selfish and egotistical, uncaring about others to the point of ruthless cruelty, and, it would seem, a failure where personal relationships were concerned, if his divorce from his wife was anything to go by. And this was the man who wanted to take her son away from her.

'Clare?'

She became aware that Jack had walked up to her. She turned and he read the naked emotions in her face. He drew in his breath sharply. Then he said in a curt undertone, 'Why? Why do you hate me so much?'

Her face lost none of its loathing. 'You know why.'

A look of contempt came into his eyes. 'You're jealous—that's it, isn't it? You can't bear to share him, to see him happy with someone other than yourself.' He gave a sound of disgust. 'Maybe it's just as well I found out about him when I did, otherwise you'd have ended up smothering him.'

She turned to walk away, but he caught her elbow. 'What's the matter, Clare? Are you too much of a coward to face the truth when you hear it?'

'I'm not going to argue with you; you're so self-centred that you only see what you want to see.'

It could have escalated into a full-blown row if Toby hadn't come up and taken hold of Clare's hand. 'Mummy, is it all right if I buy a present for Jonesy? It's his birthday soon.'

'Yes, of course.' She shook off Jack's hand and went with Toby to the souvenir shop, where he took his time over his purchase.

Jack followed them in but stood by the door, waiting. There were two female assistants in the shop, quite young; they looked like students doing the job in their spare time. They began to whisper to each other and Clare heard one say, 'I'm sure it's him. I've seen his photo in the papers.' They giggled together. 'Isn't he good-looking? And all that money!'

With a shock Clare realised they were talking about Jack. He wasn't taking any notice, although their behaviour was pretty obvious. It made Clare wonder if his sort of fame attracted women, whether they tried to make out with him. For his wealth mostly, she supposed. Although, glancing at him, she realised that he had the sort of presence that would attract women anyway, with his height, strong body and lean features.

It was strange; Clare didn't remember feeling any great attraction towards him herself when they had spent those long winter days together. Their coming together had been a sudden recognition of his desperate need for comfort, which only she could give him. But comfort had changed into passion, and something had awakened in Clare's heart that she had never felt before. In his arms that night she had felt the first stirrings of something that could have grown into a consuming flame that would have lasted all her life.

But the next morning Jack had killed that feeling stone dead when he threw her out, leaving her heart cold within her until Toby had come along to warm her into life again.

Toby finally made up his mind, paid for the model of the bridge that he'd chosen and they walked to the door. Then one of the assistants called out, 'Have you forgotten this?' and held out a model car which Toby had pulled out of his pocket with his money.

It was Jack who answered. Taking it from her, he said, 'Thank you; it belongs to my son.'

He'd used the pronoun deliberately, Clare knew that, but she surprised him by giving him a cold smile when he joined them. Though her voice was like ice when she said in a scathing undertone, *'He will never be your son.'* And she knew that she would do anything, *anything* she could to make that true.

Jack invited them to have lunch, but Clare coldly refused and he didn't push it. 'I'll call up my chauffeur to take you home.'

'Thanks, but we'll take a cab.'

There were plenty of cruising taxis; Clare only had to lift an arm and one pulled in beside them. Jack gave her a rather bitter look, but Clare ignored it. She went to hurry Toby along, but the boy tilted his head to Jack and said with formal politeness, 'Thank you very much for taking Mummy and me out.'

Ruffling his hair, Jack grinned and said, 'That's OK, Toby. See you next week.'

'Where will we go?'

Tapping his finger against Toby's nose, Jack said, 'Wait and see. It's a surprise.'

Toby immediately smiled with pleasure, and, getting into the cab, climbed on the back seat so that he could wave to Jack through the window.

Inwardly seething, Clare was about to direct the driver to the flat, but then remembered that she'd allowed Tanya and her boyfriend to meet there, so told him to take her to her shop instead. There she immediately picked up the phone and called Paul.

'Simmer down,' he soothed when she started to angrily describe the morning. 'I'll come over and pick you up. Take you both out to lunch.'

'I ought not to,' Clare said with a sigh. 'I have loads of work to do.'

'OK, so I'll bring along a sandwich or something and we'll have it there.'

Paul's idea of 'a sandwich' was to call in at Harrods on the way over and select a hamper full of luxurious goodies. It suited Clare, who liked pâté, cold chicken and beluga caviare, all washed down with champagne, but Toby only picked at the food, and informed Paul that his daddy didn't have to have funny food because he knew how to order a take-away pizza. Having made this devastating comment, Toby left them in Clare's office and went into the shop, where he was the spoilt darling of all the female staff.

'It seems that Straker has made a hit with Toby,' Paul remarked dryly.

Clare nodded, unable to deny it. 'But I don't want them to get too close,' she said in frustration. 'I've got to think of some way of making the court change its mind about access rights. If Jack could get involved in a really juicy scandal it might help,' she murmured wistfully.

'It's hardly likely. The only scandal, if you can call it that, was his divorce.'

She looked at him with curiosity. 'Was it much of a scandal? I don't remember reading anything about it.'

'No, I don't think it was reported much, but that was only because Straker made an immense payment to buy her off. She was out for everything she could get, apparently. But I don't think there was anyone else involved—nothing sordid,' he said, almost regretfully. 'He just wanted to be rid of her, I think.'

'There must be something shady. How about his business dealings? Have you heard any whispers of bribery and corruption?'

'Unfortunately, no.' Paul looked away to spread caviare onto a wafer-thin water biscuit. 'He's squeaky clean.'

'There must be something in his private life, then. Some secret romance. Perhaps I could hire a private detective to watch him.'

'Well, I hate to say it, Clare, but *you* were the dark secret in Straker's life.'

Put like that, it surprised her for a minute. If Jack's reputation was so clean it must have taken real desperation on his part to have let the world into the secret of his adultery and his illegitimate son. If she'd talked to Jack right from the start it might not have become public, of course. It had been her intractability that had forced him into going to court. Clare pushed that uneasy thought aside and said forcefully, 'I have *got* to do something. I just can't tolerate this situation any longer.'

'Well, there is one thing you can do, of course.'

'What's that?'

Paul was reaching out to refill her glass, and didn't look at her as he said, 'You could get married.'

'I don't want to get married.'

'Not even to keep Toby away from Straker?'

'Put like that, it's certainly an idea.' Clare picked up her glass and laughed. 'But I can hardly see any man being willing to marry me for that reason.'

Picking up his own glass, Paul looked at her over its rim. 'I would.'

For a moment Clare thought he was joking and started to smile, but as she looked into his eyes the smile slowly faded. 'You mean it!'

'I would hardly have suggested it otherwise.'

'But...' She stopped.

'Oh, I know there are lots of buts. *But* you're not in love with me. *But* you don't want to be tied down by marriage and a husband. And the biggest but is probably that you don't even fancy me—sexually, I mean.' Clare flushed a little and looked away, her silence telling him he was right. His face tightened a little, but he went on. 'I'm fully aware of all that. But

I'm willing to take only what you wish to give in exchange for your companionship and the chance to help you and Toby.'

'That's very—altruistic of you, Paul.' Clare gave him a shrewd look. 'And the fact that you'd definitely be scoring off Straker where it hurts him most doesn't come into it, I suppose?'

Paul smiled. 'I must admit, the deliciousness of that idea had crossed my mind,' he agreed.

Her face growing thoughtful, Clare said, 'I suppose it would be the stable family background that the judge said Toby needed. And maybe we needn't get married; we could just get engaged.'

'That might work for a while,' Paul agreed. 'But not indefinitely, obviously.'

'No. But if Jack was convinced that he wouldn't be able to get any more access to Toby than he has already then he might drop the whole thing,' Clare suggested, becoming excited by the idea.

'That is certainly a thought. Although I can't see him giving up so easily,' Paul warned, seeing his offer being belittled.

Clare raised shining eyes to his. 'Oh, Paul, do you really think it might work?' But then she shook her head. 'But I can't let you do it. Surely you want a real marriage? It wouldn't be fair to you. I couldn't possibly—'

'I wouldn't have made the offer if I hadn't wanted to,' he pointed out.

She stared at him, trying to figure out all the implications, then said slowly, 'I'm very, very grateful, Paul. I want you to know that. But I must think it through.'

'There wouldn't be any strings, any obligation to show your gratitude on your part, if that's what you're thinking,' he said bluntly.

Her eyes widened. 'You'd be content with that?'

'If that's all you're prepared to give, then, yes.'

A troubled look came into Clare's eyes. 'I'm not sure about this. I'd like to think it over.'

'Of course.' He stood up. 'Let me know when you come to a decision.'

He went to leave, but she caught his hand. 'I'm really very grateful, Paul.'

Clare lay awake most of that night, going over the idea, wondering if it would work. She had never really fallen in love, was beginning to think that she never would, and she certainly didn't want to get married just for the sake of it. But if it meant keeping Toby away from Jack...

So if Paul was willing to help her why shouldn't she accept his offer? He had said that there would be no strings, but she didn't believe him. Clare had noticed the way Paul eyed her sometimes, and knew that he wanted her. Before long he would make that need known and she would have little choice but to go to bed with him. Well, OK, that wouldn't be too high a price to pay for control of Toby's future, for peace of mind. Paul didn't turn her on, but then nor did any other man that she knew. She hadn't felt any desperate sexual need, not since... Clare gripped her hands into fists. Not since Jack had used her.

Pushing that thought out of her mind, Clare tried to concentrate on Paul. She was shrewd enough to know that Paul would probably get as much out of the deal as she would—scoring off Jack being the biggest satisfaction. He would enjoy flaunting his triumph among his business colleagues, showing her off and helping her to make it as difficult as possible for Jack to get near Toby, because that was what would hurt Jack most. All Clare wanted was for Jack to stay away from them, and that she wanted more than anything in the world. So if marrying Paul would make it possible, then why not take advantage of his offer?

Having convinced herself that it would be ridiculous not to, Clare called Paul the next day and accepted. Within an hour what seemed like a whole florist's shop of flowers arrived, even though it was Sunday, closely followed by Paul, loaded up with presents for them both. For Toby there were toys, and for Clare a beautiful old diamond and ruby ring. Paul had been busy, using his influence to get the gifts for them, letting her see that he had the power. They had champagne to celebrate, and Clare tried to explain to Toby that Paul was going to be his new daddy.

'But I've got a new daddy,' he objected. 'Are you allowed to have two?'

'Perhaps it might be best if I continued as an uncle for the time being,' Paul suggested smoothly.

He only stayed for an hour, and when he'd gone Toby sat among his new and expensive toys, looking at Clare with an anxious frown. 'Does Paul have to be my new daddy? I like Mr Straker best.'

'But you've known Paul a lot longer, honey. And he's very nice.'

Pushing the toys aside, Toby got out his colouring pencils and went to sit at the table. 'I'm going to draw a picture for my *real* daddy,' he announced.

*   *   *

The announcement of their engagement appeared in the quality papers the next morning and was immediately picked up by the tabloids. Clare had gone to the sale preview of the contents of a house in the country and knew nothing about it until she contacted her staff, who told her that reporters had been phoning all day. 'They even camped out on the pavement outside the shop,' her assistant informed her with some relish. 'The police had to come and move them along. And the caretaker at the flats rang to say some have turned up there too.'

'Oh, Lord.' Clare groaned, but knew that she had only to get through the next couple of days and the press would leave her alone; the hectic search for news would send the hounds baying after some other poor victim before too long. She drove straight to Toby's school and picked him up in the car, but they had to run the gauntlet of reporters at the flat.

Clare had a firm hold of Toby's hand and hurried forward, but a couple of the photographers were really pushy, letting flashes off in their faces and trying to bar their way to the entrance. The caretaker was on the watch and came to open the doors for her, but Clare found herself hemmed in, with a woman shouting almost in her face, 'What does Jack Straker have to say about your engagement?'

'He says mind your own damn business.' Jack's curt voice sounded behind her, and suddenly Toby was scooped up from the ground, a wide pair of shoulders was clearing the way and then they were through the doors, which the caretaker slammed shut in the faces of the reporters.

Clare turned to take Toby from Jack but drew back,

feeling a sudden shiver of apprehension as she saw cold, dark anger in his eyes.

The entrance doors were of glass and the cameras were still flashing. Taking hold of her wrist, and still carrying Toby, Jack propelled her towards the stairs and ran up them, not slowing down until they reached the door of her flat.

'I'll take him now.'

Clare reached for Toby, but Jack said harshly, 'Open the door.'

She opened her mouth to argue, saw his eyes again and did as he'd ordered.

Toby was clinging tightly to Jack's neck, not quite sure whether to be upset or to think of the whole episode as an adventure. Gently Jack disengaged his hands and set him down. 'Hey, that's a good drawing.' He pointed to the one on the table. 'Is that for me?'

'Yes, but it isn't finished yet.'

'Show me.'

Jack was almost rigid with anger, but somehow he managed to control it as he soothed the boy. But having to do it in no way soothed his own fury, only serving to fuel it instead. Glancing at Clare malevolently, he saw her toss her head, the rich dark hair loose and swirling. There was a look of defiance in her eyes, even though she, too, made a fuss of Toby, getting him a drink, playing down the scuffle with the reporters.

Only when Toby was fully absorbed in his drawing did Jack get to his feet, walk into the kitchen and lean against the wall, arms folded as he waited, grim-faced, for Clare to follow him.

She did so reluctantly, shutting the door so that Toby wouldn't hear. 'All right,' she said acidly. 'Just say what you came to say and then go.'

'If you think I'm going to let you get away with this that easily, then you're very much mistaken,' he said grimly. Thrusting himself off the wall, he strode forward and loomed over her, being deliberately intimidating. 'How the hell could you stoop to this?'

'To what are you——?'

'You know damn well to what! To getting engaged to someone you don't love just to spite me.'

Because the accusation was true, Clare overreacted and said with stiff-necked stubbornness, 'You're completely wrong; I'm mad about Paul.'

'Oh, you're mad all right—mad at me for getting even the little access I've been granted to Toby.' Jack's face filled with contempt. 'I never believed that you could be so vindictive.'

Colour came into Clare's cheeks, but her voice was cold as she said, 'You know nothing about me.'

His eyes narrowing, Jack said, 'Obviously not.' His clenched fists were in his pockets as he strove for self-control, the material drawn tight across his hips. 'But one thing I do know—Paul Venton is entirely the wrong man to be Toby's stepfather—and equally the wrong man to be your husband!' he said bluntly.

'How dare you? Paul is a kind, educated, civilised man who will make an excellent husband and father.'

'Rubbish!' Jack's hands came out of his pockets. 'The only reason he's offered to marry you is because he's my rival, my enemy! Had he asked you to marry him before I showed up? Well, had he?'

'Mind your own damn business!'

'Which means he hadn't,' Jack sneered. Unable to stop himself, he put his hand on her upper arm, gripping her through the thin silk of her blouse, his anger so intense that Clare could feel it. 'Can't you see that he's doing this to get at me? He's using you, Clare.'

Her face went white. 'Well, you should know,' she said viciously. 'You're an expert at using people.'

Jack stared at her, taken aback by the naked fury in her face, a fury that was close to hatred. But then swift comprehension came into his eyes. 'Is that what you think? That I was just using you all those years ago? Is that why you hate me?'

'It would seem a good enough reason.' Clare tried to pull away, but he wouldn't let go.

'You couldn't be more wrong.' He took hold of her other arm, his face intent. 'What happened between us was—'

'Was sex,' Clare cut in contemptuously. 'But not pure and not simple. I was there and you used me.'

'I don't remember you fighting me off,' Jack accused. 'In fact you seemed to take quite a lot of pleasure in it. More than once,' he added maliciously.

'But you were the one who suddenly remembered you had a wife and threw me out the next morning.'

She was too angry to guard her feelings and there was a note of such bitterness in her voice that Jack couldn't help but recognise it. He frowned, stared at her intently. Gropingly he said, 'What are you saying? That it was more for you than just sex? Is that why you're so—?'

Suddenly afraid that she'd given herself away, that he would read her inmost feelings, Clare put her hands flat against his chest and tried to push him away. But she might as well have tried to push down a stone wall; Jack's grip only tightened. Flustered, she took refuge in attack and said, 'Don't be so ridiculous! It meant nothing to me. Less than nothing.'

'I don't believe you.'

'It's true!'

Gazing down at her, Jack's eyes narrowed. 'Well, there's only one way to find out.' And, pulling her roughly against him, he bent his head to kiss her.

For a moment Clare was too stunned to struggle but then, as the warm hardness of his lips reached her, she began to desperately fight him off. He had her arms pinned to her sides, but she tried to move her head away, tossing it furiously, cursing him, her eyes wild. She managed to kick him once, but he only bent her backwards so that she needed to brace her legs in order not to fall.

'You rat!' Clare managed to move her mouth away long enough to swear at him, but then he pulled her close again and cut off the furious words. She bit him, and laughed with satisfaction when she felt him wince, but then his lips were hard against her own, forcing her mouth open, restricting all movement.

Tears of rage came into Clare's eyes as she fought not only Jack but soon the insidious sensations that were growing deep inside her. She felt them, knew them for what they were—old enemies that she'd thought conquered long ago, but which now returned a hundred times as strong, trying to seduce her senses, trying to make her surrender to the desire and fulfilment she had only known in his arms.

With a tremendous effort, Clare managed to jerk

her head away just long enough to shout, 'Toby!' on a high, panic-stricken note.

Her son, in the best tradition of white knights, came flying to her rescue. He ran into the kitchen and stopped in surprise, uncertain what to do. But Jack took no notice. He was staring down at Clare with the strangest look in his grey eyes, as if for a moment he was too stunned to react.

'Let me go,' Clare ordered, the wild, frightened look still in her eyes, her cheeks flushed and her hair dishevelled.

Jack blinked, his thoughts chaotic, but instead of doing as she asked he pulled her to him and again kissed her. But there was no hardness in his mouth now—instead it was soft, exploring, as if he were trying to reach her soul. And it was therefore all the more dangerous. Clare gave a whimper of despair. 'No!'

Two small hands gripped Jack's trouser-leg and tried to pull him away. Then Toby began to pummel him. 'Leave my mummy alone!'

Slowly, reluctantly, Jack let her go. For a long moment they just stared into each other's eyes, then Jack scooped Toby up in his arms and lifted him high over his head. He laughed and said, 'Hey, you little demon,' as he avoided Toby's still flailing fists. 'All right; I promise I won't kiss your mummy again.' Jack's eyes went to Clare and he added softly, 'Until she wants me to, that is.'

'Which will be never,' Clare said crisply. 'Now, get out.'

But the grey eyes continued to study her before

Jack finally gave Toby a hug and then set him down. 'About Paul Venton,' he began. 'You mustn't—'

'Paul and I are going to be married,' Clare said tightly. 'Just as soon as it can be arranged.'

Seeing that any argument would only make her more adamant, Jack wisely left it alone. But his face was troubled as he finally left the flat. He had a lot to think about—and it wasn't all about Clare's engagement.

After she'd put Toby to bed that evening, Clare hurried into her own room and stripped off her clothes. Jack's kiss had been an intrusion, an invasion of her senses as well as an assault on her person. In the few hours since it had happened she had been able to think of little else. She felt restless and agitated, the flame Jack had lit still a disturbing heat that she needed to drown under a cold shower. She moved to go to the bathroom, but caught sight of herself in the long mirror on the wardrobe door. Was that a bruise on her arm? Moving closer to look, she saw that it was.

She remembered how angry Jack had been when he'd held her—because she'd got engaged to his rival, presumably. But there had been something more in that kiss. Maybe it had started off in anger, in a challenge, but that wasn't the way it had ended. Closing her eyes, Clare could almost feel it again. Putting her hands on her shoulders, her head tilted back and her eyes still shut, she let them slowly slide down her length, over her breasts, her waist and on down her hips.

She let out her breath in something close to a moan, her lips parted in an ache of yearning. It had been so long; she had almost forgotten what it was like to be with a man. She wasn't into sex just to satisfy frustration, and somehow she had never met anyone she really fancied enough to go to bed with. There had been no great passion in her life, only the humiliation of being thrown out by Jack on that morning when the world had, for a few hours, seemed a very wonderful place.

Was it because she was afraid of being humiliated again that she had never taken the risk of becoming involved, never let herself want another man? Clare sighed and opened her eyes. Her body looked pretty good in the lamplight, the soft curves casting shadows, her legs long and her waist slender. Better than it had looked when she'd first met Jack all those years ago. She'd been too thin then. A teenage waif, lost and afraid. But now she was a mature woman in charge of her own destiny, a mother—and about to become a wife.

She thought of Paul. Pictured Paul running his hands over the body she could see in the mirror, wanting it, making love to it... And it was then that she suddenly turned and ran into the bathroom, where she stood under the shower until the water eventually ran cold and she had to come out at last.

The tabloid press had gone to town with the story; the next morning there were pictures of Jack pushing her into the flat in nearly all the newspapers. Clare took refuge in the office above her shop, but even there the phone seldom stopped ringing. Her assistant fielded calls from dozens of reporters, from magazines wanting interviews, from a women's group wanting her support, from members of the general public who just wanted to tell her what they thought—some for, some outspokenly against, and even one from a man who wanted to ghostwrite her story and sell it to a film company.

But one and all they wanted something from her, to feed on her ephemeral notoriety to their own advantage or that of their pet cause. None of them thought of her, that she might want to safeguard her privacy and that of her son, or that by doing what they wanted it would only serve to prolong the scandal. But perhaps they wanted that, too, these opportunists, these vultures who fed on the misfortunes of others.

Clare simply refused to speak to any of them, and was rather glad that Paul was away on business for a few days.

For a couple of days longer the harassment by the press continued, but she kept as low a profile as she possibly could, and completely ignored Jack's access rights at the weekend by taking Toby down to the seaside, telling only Jonesy where she was going.

When she had reached her twenty-first birthday she had inherited money left to her by her grandparents, and she and Toby had often spent weekends by the sea or in the countryside, looking for a holiday retreat. But now Clare realised that she couldn't just choose whatever she liked; now she supposed she would have to consult Paul, out of courtesy if nothing else. She wondered if he would be content with a quaint English cottage, or whether he would be into a house in the Bahamas or a chalet in Switzerland or something equally exotic to conform to his image.

Clare bit her lip; she had no right to think like that about Paul. She liked him, respected him, and he was helping her out of an impossible situation, so why was she having these negative thoughts about him?

She came back from the weekend feeling more determined than ever to shut Jack out of their lives. He had called her flat several times over the weekend; she knew that even before she got back because she had used her remote control to listen to the answer-machine messages. But she didn't return the calls, just got her assistant to write him a terse note of explanation.

And the next Saturday, when Jack turned up at the flat to collect Toby and Clare for his permitted access, the door was opened by Jonesy, who informed him that Clare had deputed him to go with Toby. They went to see the Thames Barrier, where Jonesy was content to doze at the teashop, so Jack had the boy to himself. It was a novel and wonderful experience for them both, but Jack felt strangely that there was something missing, and knew that it was Clare. 'Has your mummy gone out with Paul?' he couldn't resist asking Toby.

'Yes.' Toby gave Jack a contemplative look that held a hint of satisfaction. 'But she won't be able to marry him now, will she?'

'Why not?'

'Well, she can't now that you've kissed her, can she?' Toby replied with devastatingly innocent logic.

Jack blinked, then gave a shout of laughter. 'Come on, young man. I think I'd better take you for an ice cream.'

He wondered when and, disturbingly, even *if* he would see Clare again. But he saw both her and Paul only a few days later. It was at the annual dinner given by the Lord Mayor of London at the Guildhall, a glittering occasion to which most of the influential men in the city were invited, along with their wives. Jack saw Paul first; he was standing alone in the ante-room when Jack arrived, and gave a smile that was more of a smirk when he greeted Jack with overdone good humour that was far removed from the with-drawn politeness he normally used towards him. 'Ah, Straker. I hear you don't approve of my engagement.'

'No,' Jack agreed evenly.

'But you mustn't worry, old boy. I'll take good care of Toby; see he gets a good education and all that.'

Paul was deliberately rubbing in his victory, mak-ing the most of what he was certain must be Jack's deep chagrin. Perhaps he was even trying to goad him into making some unwise comment or action. But to Paul's surprise Jack merely smiled and said, 'Oh, I'm not in the least worried about that.'

Paul went to say something further but saw that Jack was looking past him, his eyes arrested. He turned to follow his gaze and saw that Clare was walking towards them from the cloakroom. She looked stunning. She wore a deep red evening dress with beaded shoulder-straps, the skirt slit high at the sides so that the long length of her shapely legs could be glimpsed as she walked. Her hair was drawn back and she looked cool, classy and sophisticated—a woman any man would be proud to be seen with.

Paul made the most of it, possessively catching her hand and carrying it lightly to his lips as she reached him. Clare glanced at him, gave a small smile, but then her eyes went to Jack. There was a slightly strained look in her face, he noticed, but wasn't to know that it was because her heart had jumped at sight of him, and that it had taken a great effort to walk towards them so coolly.

Still holding Clare's hand, Paul lifted it so that Jack couldn't help but notice the ring, with its huge ruby in the centre, that she wore on her engagement finger. 'You're looking at Clare's ring,' Paul remarked with satisfaction. 'It's antique, of course.'

Jack lifted his eyes, his expression giving nothing away. 'Couldn't you afford a new one?' he asked silkily, then moved away before Paul could think of an answer.

But a few minutes later Jack was standing with another group of lone men, talking cricket, when he saw Paul and Clare walk past. Clare was wearing silver high-heeled shoes, the back just a slender strap holding them in place and revealing her ankles. They were very slim, shapely ankles, and Jack found himself wondering just why he'd never noticed them before. Somebody asked him a question but he didn't reply, his gaze rapt, his thoughts far away.

They were seated at opposite sides of the huge banqueting hall during dinner, which was a long-drawn-out affair with many courses and even more speeches at the end. It was during one of the earlier speeches that Jack saw one of the liveried footmen come into the room and hand Clare a message. Straining to watch, he saw Clare say something to Paul and start to rise, but Paul pulled her back. They seemed to have a short, whispered argument, then Clare determinedly got to her feet and discreetly left the room. Paul didn't follow; he sat on with a set, angry look on his face. Immediately Jack excused himself to his neighbours and went after Clare. He caught her up in the entrance where she was putting on her coat and asking the doorman to find her a taxi.

'What is it?' he asked sharply as he came up to her. 'Is there something wrong with Toby?'

She looked at him in surprise, then shook her head. 'No, it's Jonesy. It's his birthday and he's gone on a drinking bout. I've got to find him before the police do. The authorities have threatened to throw him out of the hostel if he gets arrested again.' She looked round impatiently. 'I must get a cab.'

'Where are you going to look for him?'

'There are some pubs he goes to. And down by the river—there are some places where people live rough; he might be with them.'

A taxi came into sight and the doorman lifted an arm to hail it for her, but Jack said firmly, 'No. You can't possibly go to those sort of areas alone—and definitely not dressed like that. We'll take my car.'

'But I haven't got time to—'

But Jack was already on his mobile, calling up his car, and within a couple of minutes it pulled up at the kerb. 'I'll drive myself,' Jack told his chauffeur, and took the man's place in the driving seat. 'Where first?' he asked crisply.

Clare gave him the name of the first pub and told him where it was. He drove well, safely, but with a sure knowledge of London and its traffic that enabled him to take advantage of backstreets and whip through the lanes of queuing cars. They reached the

pub and Clare went to get out, but Jack said, 'No, I'll
go. Wait here.'

She didn't argue; it was the sort of pub mainly pa-
tronised by working men and down-and-outs—a place
where the arrival of any even passable-looking
woman would have raised some lewd remarks, if not
outright propositions. Jack put an overcoat over his
evening suit before he went in, and was back within
a few minutes. 'He's not there, and the landlord hasn't
seen him.'

They went on to four more pubs, but without success. 'Then it's cardboard city,' Clare said with a sigh.
'That damn woman at the hostel! I could strangle her.'

'What woman?'

'Some do-gooder who comes there occasionally to
help out. I gave Jonesy a bottle of malt whisky to
drink in his room, so that he wouldn't go out and get
into trouble. But this woman saw it and took it from
him, said it was against the rules. So, of course, he
went out to get drunk instead.'

'Does he *have* to get drunk?' Jack asked mildly.

'Yes. It used to be a very special day for him and
his wife. It was also the day they met and the day
they married. His wife used to make a big thing of it,
and they always went out to celebrate. It was the high-
light of their year. Now he can't bear to remember,
so he gets drunk to forget. I don't expect you to understand that, but—'

'Don't be silly,' Jack cut in. 'There have been a
great many times when I've been tempted to drown
my sorrows.'

Clare glanced at his profile, his strong, lean face
outlined by the passing street lights as he concentrated

on driving. She realised that she knew little about his inner feelings, except where Toby was concerned. Was it loneliness that drove him towards his son? she wondered. And did those occasions on which he felt like getting drunk include the days when he missed his wife? The knowledge that he would resist temptation, that he would never give in to unhappiness, was suddenly certain in her mind. But wouldn't that make the agony of mind, of heart, even harder to bear? Then she remembered that he had turned to her for solace when his father had died—so who had he turned to when he got divorced?

They reached the dark streets where the main railway line crossed them overhead, slicing through the city, carried along on hundreds of arched bridges under which the homeless had made their own, private city. Jack pulled up a short distance from the first place, and Clare followed him out of the car.

'I'm coming with you,' she said before he could protest. 'I've been here before looking for Jonesy. And some of the men used to live in the hostel. They know me, and they'll talk to me.'

Looking at the set of her chin, Jack knew that she wasn't going to back down. He didn't waste any time in futile argument, instead saying, 'All right, but take that bauble off your finger.'

Clare put the 'bauble' into her evening bag and locked it in the car, then pulled her coat close around her as they hurried down the street and approached the first of the pile of cardboard boxes that was some unfortunate person's home. Their polite approach and obvious concern for one of their own made the people helpful, but none of them remembered seeing Jonesy.

It was the same at the next two places, but at the fourth they had some luck at last—a man who had used to live at the hostel remembered seeing Jonesy on the Embankment, the long walkway that bordered the river Thames.

They hurried back to the car and Jack drove slowly along, looking for the old man on one of the ornate iron benches. Finally they spotted him—just as two policemen were approaching him from the opposite direction!

'There he is! Stop!' Clare sprang out of the car before it had hardly stopped moving, ran over to Jonesy and grabbed the bottle out of his hand, tossing it over the wall into the river. Then she pushed him upright and sat beside him, supporting his weight as the policemen came along.

'Having trouble, miss?' one asked.

'No, just enjoying the night air,' Clare returned calmly.

The policeman looked at Jonesy suspiciously, who didn't help by opening one eye and announcing in a drunken slur, 'Today is my birthday, young man.'

'Many happy returns, sir.' The policeman leant forward to smell his breath, but Clare put her arm across Jonesy's face. 'My father has a cold; I'm sure you don't want to catch it.'

Strolling up, Jack said in a solicitous voice, 'Is your father feeling better now, darling? Shall we take him home?' Then he looked at the policemen. 'Rotten to have a cold when you're elderly, isn't it? The poor man got a bit over-heated and came outside to cool down.' With a careless hand Jack indicated the prestigious Savoy Hotel behind him, for all the world as if they'd spent the evening there. 'Better drive him back, I think.' He smiled at the policemen. 'Perhaps you wouldn't mind giving me a hand with the poor old thing?'

It must have been something in Jack's manner, because the two policemen helped to get Jonesy into the back of the car before wishing them a respectful goodnight.

When they were driving safely away, Jack said in appalled tones, 'My God, Clare, he reeks of cheap wine!'

Clare gave a peal of delighted laughter. 'I know, I know. Oh, do you think they really believed we were dining at the Savoy with him?'

'With Jonesy in those rags of his? Impossible.' But he gave a huge grin. 'I'm just glad they didn't insist on helping us back into the hotel!'

'Perhaps they thought he was an eccentric millionaire. Oh, but thank goodness we got to him in time. He would have hated to wake up in a police cell again, poor old love, and to have lost his bed at the hostel even more. He can sleep it off at my place, and tomorrow he can go back with no one any the wiser.'

'You're really fond of him, aren't you?' Jack was driving much more slowly now, and was able to glance at her. 'You even pretended he was your father. But what about your own parents? You never talk about them.'

Clare was silent for a moment, remembering that Jack was her enemy, but then she gave a small shrug and said, 'Because I don't remember them. They were killed in an accident when I was very young and I was brought up by my grandparents, who were pretty ancient. That was OK, I loved them dearly and they understood me, but when they in turn died I was passed on to live with a great-aunt and uncle who'd never had any children.'

She paused, and Jack said, 'Was it tough? Was that why you ran away?'

'Yes. I was very unhappy. There were constant battles because of their antediluvian ideals and my need to have some independence, be my own person. So I ran away to London and slept rough, like those people in cardboard city, when my money ran out.' She looked to see if she'd shocked him, but Jack's profile gave nothing away. 'That's where I got in your car, that time, in London. You drove nearly all the way to your father's place without knowing I was there.' But that made her remember other things, and she said stiltedly, 'It was kind of you to help me tonight.'

'I like Jonesy.' When she didn't speak, Jack said, 'Paul didn't want you to look for him, did he?'

'He wanted me to wait,' Clare corrected. 'He was due to give a speech and wanted me to hear it.'

'Good Lord!' Jack exclaimed. 'So was I. I'd forgotten all about it.' Clare expected him to be annoyed, but he only laughed and said, 'They'll probably never invite me again.'

'Would you mind?' she asked curiously.

'I'll live. But will you—having chosen Jonesy before Paul?'

'It was hardly that,' Clare protested, but then she gave a small laugh. 'But you're right; he doesn't approve of Jonesy very much.'

'So what will happen about him—when you're married?'

'It hasn't been discussed,' Clare answered coolly, and pointedly changed the subject. 'Will you help me to get him up to my flat?'

'Yes, of course. Who's looking after Toby tonight?'

'He's staying at the home of one of his friends.'

When they reached the flat Clare thought they were going to have a struggle getting Jonesy upstairs, but Jack simply heaved him up into his arms and carried him. The old man was, admittedly, thin and wiry, but even so it must have taken a great deal of strength to do it. They put him to bed in Toby's room, Clare waiting in the sitting-room while Jack undressed him.

'He'll be OK now,' he told her. 'Although he'll probably have the world's worst hangover when he wakes up.'

Again Clare was polite. 'It was very kind of you. I expect you'd like to get back to the banquet.'

'Surely it's about over by now?' Jack gave her an amused look, knowing that she wanted him to leave but was unable to come right out and say it because she had to be grateful to him. Taking off his coat and sitting down comfortably in an armchair, he added, 'I imagine we'll have your fiancé turning up any time now, spitting fire and brimstone, turning proverbially green with jealousy to find me here.'

'So maybe it would be a good idea if he didn't find you here,' she pointed out.

He stretched out his legs. 'A coffee would be nice. I missed out on it, you may remember.'

Clare didn't move. 'Are you determined to make trouble for me?'

'Oh, but I'm saving you from trouble.' Clare raised an eloquently disbelieving eyebrow. 'The trouble of going through a divorce in a couple of years' time when you find you just can't stand living with Venton any longer,' he explained equably.

Clare's face hardened. 'That won't happen.'

'Who're you trying to convince, Clare? It certainly isn't me.'

'Is that why you helped me with Jonesy—just to make trouble with Paul?'

Jack didn't answer, but instead pointed with his neatly-shod foot at a box containing an expensive remote-controlled car that Paul had bought for Toby. 'That looks new; did you buy it for Toby?' His eyes held hers. 'Or was it Paul?'

'He gave it to him to mark our engagement,' Clare admitted.

'I thought you didn't want the boy to be spoiled by expensive presents. Didn't want his affection to be bought—that was, I think, the expression you used at the hearing.'

'It was a one-off,' she said defensively, uneasy about that aspect herself, but feeling that she couldn't do a great deal until after she and Paul were married.

'So Venton is allowed to buy him presents but I'm not, is that it?' Jack asked on a grim note.

'Paul *is* going to be Toby's stepfather.'

His voice hardening, Jack said, 'And I just happen to be his natural father.'

'Yes,' Clare agreed, rising to her feet, her own voice becoming cold. 'It just happened. It certainly wasn't planned. I didn't choose you to be Toby's father—as I have chosen Paul.'

God! Jack thought, she looks fantastic when she's angry—almost as good as she looks when she's happy. And he tried to remember how she'd looked when they'd been together in his father's house and she'd gone to bed with him—but he found to his surprise that that girl had gone from his mind and been entirely replaced by this beautiful, vital creature. And he had driven her into the arms of that fool, Paul Venton.

Before it had been just a fight to get near Toby, but now Jack knew that there was no way he was going to let Clare throw herself away on his rival. He glanced at her, wondering why it was that people couldn't read each other's thoughts when they were as strong as his. But Clare was watching him, almost warily, and he merely gave a twisted smile and said hopefully, 'Coffee?'

With an exasperated sigh, Clare went into the kitchen to make it, and it was while she was there that Paul arrived. Jack, damn him, went to the entry-phone and let him in. Thankfully, Paul played it cool. When he came into the kitchen she was prepared for anything, but Paul came over and kissed her, saying, 'Did you find Jonesy?'

'Yes, he's asleep in Toby's room.'

'Good! Good. I'm so pleased. I just had to stay and give the speech, you know.'

'Yes. Did you have to make it longer to make up for Jack not being there to give his?' she asked sweetly.

Paul smiled. 'I was quite confident that you were capable of managing on your own.'

Clare laughed, rather liking that neat answer. 'Would you like a coffee?'

'Please.'

He carried the tray into the sitting-room for her and they sat down, for all the world as if this were some friendly tea-party.

'Our host wasn't too pleased with your dashing off without a word of explanation or apology,' Paul remarked to Jack.

'I'm sure they'll understand that it was an emergency,' Jack responded casually.

After taking a sip of his coffee, Paul said, 'Clare and I have great plans for Toby, don't we, darling? But we will, of course, make a point of keeping you informed. After all, we want to be civilised about this.'

'Really?' Jack was at his most sardonic.

'Yes. He'll go to the very best school, of course, then university, and hopefully will come into my company with me.'

Clare blinked, not having been told anything of Paul's plans. She caught Jack's eye and knew from the curl of his lip exactly what he was thinking. As lightly as she could, she said, 'I hardly think it necessary to map out Toby's life when he's so young. He might have ideas of his own when he gets older.'

Jack laughed harshly. 'He won't get a chance to think for himself. Because it would give Venton the greatest pleasure to turn my son against me—and what a climax if he could set Toby up as my business rival! And that's what he's looking for; that would be the ultimate revenge, give him the most fulfilment.'

Paul laughed, knowing he had the upper hand. 'What a ridiculous—and vulgar idea.'

Draining his cup, Jack put it on the small table beside his chair and stood up. 'But then, as you never tire of telling people, I come from common, working-class stock, so what can you expect? Thanks for the coffee, Clare. Goodnight.'

She rose, saying stiffly, 'I'll see you out.'

'No need; I know the way.'

She didn't follow him; when she heard the outer door shut Clare turned on Paul. 'Is that why you're marrying me, Paul? To revenge yourself on Jack through Toby?'

'Of course not!' He gave a boyish grin. 'But I must admit that I enjoyed riling him.'

For a moment Clare studied his face, then said forcefully, 'I hope that's all it was, Paul, because there is no way I am going to allow you to use my son as some kind of pawn in a game against his father! And neither you nor Jack is going to have any say in his upbringing or his education. I appreciate your good intentions, but you may remember that the reason I agreed to marry you is so that I could have total control of my son.'

'Of course,' Paul responded at once. 'That's understood. But you must allow me to have a dig at Straker from time to time, you know. And I must say that I've never seen him so easily goaded.' He smiled, remembering, but then gave a wry frown. 'I bet it will be in the papers tomorrow that you went off with him in the middle of the Lord Mayor's banquet.'

Clare looked stricken. 'Oh, Lord, I hope not.'

Luckily, when she looked out of the window the next morning, there were no reporters waiting outside the block, so she was able to go straight to work, having arranged for the mother of Toby's friend to take the

boys to school. Jonesy she had to leave still asleep
and snoring in Toby's bed. She had a busy morning,
cleaning and pricing up a van-load of goods that she
had bought at a sale, and afterwards having lunch with
a client who had bought a late Victorian house and
wanted Clare to furnish it entirely with contemporary
furniture and fittings. The lunch was rather long, and
afterwards, instead of going back to the shop, Clare
decided instead to go home and make sure that Jonesy
was OK before picking Toby up from school.

When she got to the flat she went straight to Toby's
room, but Jonesy wasn't there; he had carefully
stripped the bed and gone. Wondering if his hangover
was as monumental as Jack had predicted, Clare went
into her own bedroom and on into the bathroom.
Opening the door, she stood transfixed. Standing in
front of her was a complete stranger, a man—and he
was stark naked!

For the most terrible moment Clare thought that she
was in the wrong flat, but then knew that she wasn't
and opened her mouth to scream.

'Don't!' the man yelled. 'I'm Tanya's boyfriend.'

Clare tried to stop the scream, but her breath caught
in her throat and she started to choke. Quickly the
man came over and thumped her unceremoniously on
the back. She coughed, spluttered, but at least could
breathe. Through watering eyes Clare looked at him
again and realised that he wasn't such a stranger after
all. 'But you—you're—' She coughed again. 'You're
Sean Munro.'

He grinned. 'Well, I hope it was only my face you
recognised.'

'Oh!' Clare blushed. 'I'll leave you to put something on.'

'It might be a good idea,' he agreed, flashing her his famously boyish grin.

She came out of the bathroom feeling dazed. Wow! No wonder Tanya had wanted somewhere discreet to meet her lover. An American, Sean Munro was an international star of film, television and stage, as chat show hosts always put it. His face was known everywhere that his films were shown, which was more or less all over the world. Even Clare, who was usually immune to fame, felt a thrill of excitement at actually meeting him in the flesh. At that thought she laughed aloud; she had indeed met him entirely in the flesh!

He came into the sitting-room some ten minutes later, fully dressed, looking just as handsome as he appeared on the screen, and with a rueful smile playing around his lips. 'Tanya left earlier. We didn't expect you back. Didn't Tanya call you to say we would be coming here today?'

Clare shook her head. 'If she called the message didn't reach me. Was there anyone else here when you arrived? An old man called Jonesy?'

'No.' Again the rueful smile. 'I guess we chose a bad day. It's real nice of you to let us borrow your place like this.'

'Not at all. I hope your "talks" are proving satisfactory,' Clare said on a sardonic note, having noticed that her bed had been remade.

Sean grinned, not at all embarrassed. 'They sure are.'

He was so open that Clare laughed. 'It must be very difficult for you both. I must admit that when Tanya asked me if she could borrow the flat, I thought she was being ultra-secretive—but now I see why it was necessary.' Without asking, he went to fix himself a drink and she gave him a contemplative look, trying to recall what she had chanced to read about him in the press. She seemed to remember that he had been divorced once before, and had separated from his second wife some time ago. Since then he had been seen with a number of beautiful women—American actresses and models mainly. It seemed out of character for him to be dating an upper class English woman— and a married one at that. Although Tanya was beautiful, too. So maybe he really was serious about her.

'How on earth did you and Tanya meet?' Clare asked as he lounged in the armchair.

'At a party in Washington. She's related to some British diplomat, and was over there visiting with his family. We got along fine. So when I came over here to make a movie, I looked her up.'

They chatted for a while longer, but then Clare had to leave to pick Toby up from school, so Sean left with her. At the entrance Clare checked that there weren't any reporters around, but Sean put on a pair of dark glasses and turned up his collar anyway, in what looked like a habitual gesture. Was he being ultra-careful to protect Tanya's reputation, or just because he was so used to being a centre of attention, his familiar features a magnet for all eyes wherever he went? Clare wondered.

She shivered, thinking that it must be a terrible way to have to live, and hardly worth all the fame. The brush with the press that she had experienced herself had already put her off for life. Clare set off to walk to the school while Sean whistled up a taxi, putting a friendly hand on her arm as they parted in another easy gesture—the sex symbol giving the women he met something to talk about, making them feel good.

That evening, Jonesy looked after Toby while Clare went out to dinner with Tanya. They chose a little French bistro off Kensington Church Street, a place they'd used a lot when they used to meet while on holiday from school. 'Tell all,' Clare commanded. And couldn't resist asking, 'Is he as fabulous as he looks?'

'I asked you that about Jack Straker and you said you couldn't remember,' Tanya pointed out.

'This is different. Sean Munro is international. So give.'

Tanya laughed, enjoying herself. 'He's very experienced.'

'Most men who've been married are very experienced—and most of those who haven't been married, if it comes to that. I take it that you got past the "talking it over" stage some time ago?'

'He is very persuasive,' Tanya admitted.

'And very good-looking.'

'And extremely rich.'

'And he's already had two failed marriages, and he only has to go out with a woman for it to be reported,' Clare pointed out. 'It isn't pleasant, Tanya. I've found that out myself in the last few weeks, and Jack and I are small fry compared to Sean.'

Tanya sighed. 'Yes, I know. It's not at all the sort of thing I'm used to. I don't know what Mummy and Daddy would say.'

'Well, at least I don't have that to worry about.'

Her friend looked at her, her head on one side. 'Are you really going to marry Paul Venton? He's quite a catch, of course.'

'I'm engaged to him.'

Tanya flicked that small fact away with a wave of her hand. 'That doesn't mean a thing. What's Paul like in bed? Better than Jack Straker?'

'I wouldn't know.'

'Clare!' Tanya looked at her in astonishment. 'How can you contemplate marrying a man without trying him out first?'

'It isn't going to be that kind of marriage.'

Tanya was silent for a moment, giving her a thoughtful look, then said, 'I see. Yes, I see it all now.'

'See what?' Clare asked uneasily.

'That until you get Jack Straker out of your system you're never going to fall in love with anyone.'

'And just how do you think I ought to go about getting him out of my system?' Clare asked wryly.

'By going to bed with him again, of course.'

Clare gave an amazed gasp. 'Are you crazy? There is no one in the world I hate more.'

'Why do you hate him so much?'

'Because he's trying to take Toby away from me, of course.'

'Is that the only reason, Clare? Is it, honestly?'

Clare remembered how devastated she had felt after Jack had kissed her, and her eyes flickered and looked away. A thousand times she had told herself that it was just sex, nothing more—a bodily craving that Jack had momentarily awakened and which could easily be subdued again. But to do so had been hard—well-nigh impossible—and there had been many times since it happened when she'd wondered what it would have been like if—

Abruptly she dragged her thoughts away, and found Tanya looking at her with a knowing look in her eyes. 'You're entirely wrong,' she said tersely. 'It's a stupid idea. I hate Jack and I'm going to marry Paul.'

And like a litany she repeated it to herself as she left the restaurant. 'I hate Jack and I'm going to marry Paul. I'm going to marry Paul.'

CHAPTER EIGHT

JACK'S face as he sat in his office was grim. His thoughts were on Clare and the threat of her forthcoming marriage. He was desperately afraid that if it took place he would only be allowed the access to Toby that he had already been granted. So there would be no holidays together and he would have no say in his upbringing. His relationship with his son would be confined to one morning a week, when they would have to try to get to know each other during the course of a visit to some place of interest—unnatural surroundings where there would be little chance to really talk, really develop a deep father-son understanding.

But Jack wasn't so easily defeated; he had found out that, for Toby's sake, he could exert moral blackmail on Clare. If he just turned up she wouldn't be openly hostile towards him if Toby was there. And there were other ways of getting to see the boy. Since he had helped Clare to look after Jonesy on his birthday, the old man had become a friend. It was he who now came to watch over Toby on their Saturday outings instead of Clare. She hadn't come along since the time he'd kissed her. Because she was still angry? Or was it Venton putting his foot down? Jack didn't think it was that; Clare was quite capable of standing up to a wimp like Venton.

At the thought of him Jack felt a surge of anger.

At the moment he was negotiating a delicate deal with
a company in the Middle East, but there had been
several hitches—false rumours about the viability of
his company had reached them, had had to be proved
wrong. One of the people he was using as an agent
had been involved in a scandal, that kind of thing.
Jack didn't as yet have any proof, but he was sure
Venton was behind it. It wouldn't be the first time.
Jack's jaw set; he was darned if a man who could
resort to shady dealings was going to be allowed anywhere near his son. Or near Clare. He found that mattered, too.

Clare had been successfully keeping her head down,
and was relieved to find that the press had found other
people to hassle. She thought the whole scandal was
over, forgotten.

She knew that Tanya and Sean were still using the
flat, often without bothering to phone first, and expected daily that Tanya would call to announce some
development in their relationship. But that call didn't
come. What came instead was a plea for help. Tanya's
voice on the phone one evening, husky with urgency,
begged, 'Clare, you've got to get me out of the most
terrible fix.'

'Why, what's happened?'

'Sean and I had arranged to go away together for
the weekend. We booked into a country house hotel,
under false names, of course. I came down ahead of
Sean, and what do you think?' Tanya paused for dra-
matic effect. 'The first person I saw when I arrived
here was an aunt of Brian's! She saw me with my
overnight case, and all I could think of was to say I

was leaving it at the hotel for a friend. So I just had to give the case to the manager and leave. And it has my name and address inside it!'

'Oh, Tanya, trust you. You were always getting into stupid scrapes. You'll just have to wait until the old dear goes away, then go and explain to the manager.'

'I can't!' Tanya wailed. 'She's been sitting in the entrance hall for ages. And Sean said we mustn't arouse any suspicion. He has a paranoia about the media finding out about us.'

'Do you want me to come and collect you?'

'No, I want you to come and pretend to be me. That is, to come and collect my case and book into the room for the night.'

'But I can't do that. I have a date with Paul.'

'Can't you break it?' Tanya begged. 'If you were going out you must already have fixed up a babysitter for Toby.'

'He's staying with his friend for the night,' Clare admitted. 'But, honestly, Tanya—'

'Please, Clare, this is a matter of life and death.'

Tanya begged and pleaded, and at last Clare gave in. She rang Paul to break the date she had with him; he wasn't too happy but had little choice.

The hotel was some way out of town, and it took her a couple of hours to get there, not arriving until almost nine. She parked the car and went inside. At least there was no one who could possibly be described as an aunt sitting in the comfortably furnished entrance hall. The manager came out when she rang the bell and Clare, using the name Tanya had given her, said, 'Hello, I'm Mrs Robinson. I have a room booked—and I believe a friend delivered a small case for me?'

'Yes, that's right.' He picked up the case from behind the desk. 'I'll show you up to your room.' It was a beautiful room on the first floor, the space mostly taken up by a large king-sized bed. 'Dinner has already been ordered to be served up here,' the man told her. 'Would you like it served now, or would you prefer to wait for Mr Robinson to arrive?'

'It's pretty late; I guess I'll have it now, please. And can you send up a bottle of champagne to go with it?' Clare added, deciding that Tanya owed her that at least.

'It has already been ordered, madam.'

The meal, sumptuous and beautifully cooked, was brought up a short time later, and Clare sat down to eat, making the best of her wasted evening as well as she could. She was just pouring out a second glass of champagne when there was a knock on the door.

Thinking it was the waiter again, she called out, 'Come in.' And then her mouth fell open as she saw Jack standing there!

He came in and shut the door. 'What's happened?' he asked tersely.

Somehow Clare managed to speak. 'What do you mean, ''what's happened''?'

Jack frowned. 'I got a call saying that you were in trouble—that you needed me.'

She continued to stare at him for a minute, but then the cogs in her brain started functioning again and Clare groaned. 'Was it a woman?'

'Yes. She said she was an old friend of yours, and that you'd asked her to call me. She said she couldn't

help, that it had to be a man and that you needed me.'
Jack was studying her face, saw the chagrin and anger
in it. 'I take it there isn't an emergency?'

'No,' Clare admitted bitterly. 'It was a so-called
friend of mine, who decided to meddle in my affairs.'

'Which—*affair*—in particular?'

Clare flushed. 'It isn't what you think. We—I've
been set up.'

'So tell me.' Jack came over and helped himself to
a glass of champagne.

'How did you find the room?'

'Your friend told me to say I was Mr Robinson and
to go straight up.'

'I will strangle Tanya the next time I see her,' Clare
said with intense feeling.

'So just why did she set us—you—up?'

'Well, you see...' Clare realised it was going to be
impossible to explain. 'She just got hold of the wrong
idea, that's all.'

'Really?' Taking off his jacket, Jack put it on the
back of a chair. 'I take it that food is for Mr and Mrs
Robinson?' And when Clare reluctantly nodded he
smiled. 'Good. I haven't had dinner yet.' He sat down
and helped himself. 'Now you can tell me all about
it.'

'No,' Clare stated positively. 'I can't. Just take it
from me that it's all a very stupid mistake.' She got
to her feet. 'I'm sorry that you've been involved. Eat
what you like and use the room, if you want. I'm
going back to London.'

'Not until you've explained, you're not.' Jack
spoke calmly, but there was steely determination in
his eyes.

'I've told you; there's nothing to explain. Tanya just got the wrong idea.'

'What idea?'

She gave him an antagonistic look. 'Nothing that concerns you.'

His eyes, speculative and slightly amused, she noticed, studied her flushed face. 'I see. Well, you might as well sit down and finish your meal. I think you owe it to me to keep me company, don't you?'

'I don't owe you a thing. This wasn't my idea.'

'Ah, no, it was the wrong idea thought up by your friend. Just who is this friend?'

'We were at school together.' Reluctantly, Clare sat down opposite him, but perched on the edge of the chair all ready for flight.

'Tell me about her,' Jack commanded.

'She was always getting into scrapes. That's why I believed her when she called me this evening and—' She broke off, not wanting to give away Tanya's secret.

'And?' Jack prodded.

'She said she was in a fix and needed my help. That's why I came down here.'

His eyebrows rose, and Clare could almost see his brain working, see him using his imagination, coming to a conclusion. But was it the right one? Probably. Jack was no one's fool.

He pushed his empty plate aside, then picked up the tray and put it outside the door. When he came back he looked at her for a moment, then said, 'And is your friend truthful?'

'Not in this instance, obviously.'

'But in general?'

'Yes, I suppose so.'

His voice grew silky, almost suggestive. 'So did she mean it when she said that you needed a man—and that you wanted me?'

'No!' Clare sprang to her feet. 'Not in the way you're insinuating. Of course not. That's ridiculous.'

But Jack was also on his feet, facing her. 'That seems to be an awful lot of protests when a simple "no" would do.'

Realising that he was right, Clare took a deep breath and tried to speak calmly. 'Look, don't read something into this that isn't there. It was just an—an unfortunate choice of words on Tanya's part, that's all. Put it all down to her warped sense of humour.'

'Tanya being your friend? A close friend?'

'Yes,' Clare admitted.

'So if she's such a close friend, and presumably in your confidence, then she would know how much you hate me, wouldn't she?' He paused, watching her. 'You do still hate me, I take it?'

For answer, she gave him a belligerent look. 'You know I do.'

'So why should your close friend want to set you up with someone you hate, Clare?'

'I have no idea.' She glanced at her watch and started to say, 'I'm leaving.'

But Jack came over and put his hand on her arm. A tremor of awareness ran through her before she could get herself under control, and he felt it. 'Don't run away,' he said softly, persuasively. 'Stay and talk about Toby for a while. Is he OK? Did he enjoy himself on his school trip to the safari park?'

'Yes, he's fine. Look, I—'

'There's so much I want to know about him. All those years I missed. We've never really talked about him, have we?' As he spoke Jack led her towards a sofa and drew her down beside him. 'Tell me about him, Clare.'

She sat down reluctantly, not wanting to be with him. But his showing an interest in Toby was the surest way to her conscience. 'What do you want to know?' she asked stiltedly.

'Everything. Was he a beautiful baby? But of course he was; aren't all babies beautiful? I've been told so. Does he still believe in Father Christmas and the tooth fairy? Do you have his first tooth still?'

Clare raised surprised, green-flecked eyes to look at him. These were questions she had never imagined Jack asking. She had always thought that men took little interest in babies, that to them all that kind of thing was a woman's province. In her experience, from talking to other young mothers, fathers only became really interested in their offspring when they were old enough to take an interest in masculine things—the kind of age Toby was coming up to. It had never occurred to her that Jack might also have taken delight in all the things that had fascinated her when Toby was still a babe and a toddler.

'Yes,' she said slowly, assimilating this new facet of his character. 'He still believes that the world is a magic place.' She began to tell him things that had happened to Toby in his short life: when he'd had the measles very badly, when he'd tried to climb a tree to rescue a cat and got stuck, and they'd both had to be rescued by the fire brigade. Jack chuckled at that, his eyes lighting with amusement.

'How did you manage?' he asked. 'How did you become so successful?'

'It was the furniture and ornaments in your father's house,' she explained, to his surprise. 'I was bored and had nothing to do, so I read up about them. And when—when I came back to London I started going to car-boot sales and flea markets. I managed to pick up a few good bargains, and when Toby was born I used to take him with me, either strapped into a carrying frame or, later, in a pushchair.' She smiled reminiscently. 'He became the pet of many of the dealers; they would save little cars for him. Then I managed to get consultancy work with an auction house, and eventually started my own shop.'

'It must have been incredibly hard.' Jack put his arm along the back of the settee.

'Not really. It was fun.'

A yearning look came into Jack's eyes. 'I wish I'd—' He stopped, but then went on. 'I wish things had worked out differently, Clare.'

She didn't quite know how to take that. His hand slipped down onto her shoulder, but she moved out of his reach. 'Didn't you and your wife ever want children?'

Jack gave a small, bitter laugh. 'Are you asking me to tell you the sad saga of my marriage and divorce?'

'No, it's none of my business,' she said shortly.

But he said, 'My marriage was breaking up quite some time before I met you. We got married when I was still at university, which was a mistake in itself. I was working my way through college when I met Ruth. She was very beautiful and I fell in love with her. Fell hopelessly in love—or so I thought. Only I was too inexperienced to know that it might not last. First love is often like that for a man, I'm afraid. It entirely consumes you until you can think of nothing else. If she'd let me make love to her I might have regained my senses, but she was very clever; it was marriage or nothing.

'Even then I was quite successful in business, and she could see I was going places. She wanted to go along with me. She said she was a virgin. She wasn't,' he added shortly, and gave another cold laugh. 'She was a born prostitute; sex with her always had to be paid for one way or another. There was never any gladness, any joy in it. And certainly no spontaneity; there was too much bargaining involved for that.'

'And children?' Clare asked in a shocked voice.

'Oh, I dare say she would have condescended to have one if I'd been willing to pay a high enough price. I graduated and concentrated on building up my business, always hoping she might change. But after a few years of it I'd had enough; I was tired of the constant battle, and told her I wanted a divorce. It was then that she changed tactics. She actually came to my room one night and said that she would be every-thing I wanted, that she still loved me, wanted us to be happy. Like an optimistic fool I let her stay. A month later she told me she was pregnant. And it was soon afterwards that my father was taken ill and I met you.'

He was silent for a long moment, his face hard, his lips curled in a thin, harsh line. 'She would never have taken me into her bed to comfort me, the way you did. And I don't think she knew how to love. She was as mean with her emotions as she was with her body.

I didn't want to send you away the way I did, but I believed Ruth to be carrying my child. I was hoping that we would be fully reconciled and be able to have a normal family life. I couldn't risk jeopardising that.'

He paused again, and after a few moments Clare said gently, 'You said you "believed" she was pregnant?'

'Yes.' Jack seemed to rouse himself from a dark hole of remembrance. 'She wasn't. She'd lied about that, too. A couple of months later, after I'd been away on business, she said she'd had a miscarriage—but I didn't believe her, and dragged her to a gynaecologist. He confirmed that she'd never been pregnant. The same day I threw her out, and I've never seen her since.' His voice grew heavy with cynicism. 'But I suppose she won in the end; the divorce proved very costly.'

The bleakness in his face caught at Clare's heart. Without thinking, she put up her hand and gently stroked it across his mouth, trying to wipe away all his inner hatred and bitterness. His eyes flew to her face, but the sudden flare of desire in them frightened her and she went to snatch her hand away. But Jack caught it and held it against his mouth, then began to kiss it hungrily, the softness of his lips raining on her palm, her fingers, his teeth biting her thumb a little at the softness of its base, his tongue licking the soft skin between her fingers in exciting intimacy. And all the while his eyes held hers, telling her what could be, what he wanted.

'No!' Somehow she dragged her eyes from his and got agitatedly to her feet. But he didn't let go her hand, instead rising with her and pulling her into his arms. 'I didn't mean to touch you.'

'Didn't you? And I suppose you don't want me to kiss you again, either?'

'Certainly not!'

But there was an amused look in Jack's eyes, all mixed up with hunger and tenderness. 'Well, that's a shame, because I fully intend to do so. And I have to remind you, my sweet, that you don't have Toby to come to your rescue.'

'Don't you dare!' she threatened.

He grinned. 'Now, that was a very silly thing to say.'

Clare's eyes flashed fire. 'I shan't respond.'

His lips touched hers in gentle, insinuating exploration. 'Of course not,' he agreed. 'That's understood.'

'You'll just stand there like a fool.'

'Mmm.' His lips hardened a little, and he pulled her closer against him so that she could feel the strength of him, the heat of his body.

Clare kept her lips firmly closed, her body stiff with defiance. His lips did to her mouth what he had done to her hand—kissing, biting gently, his tongue seeking a way in, sending shock waves of desire running through her that she tried desperately to hide. But then his lips moved from her mouth to her throat, and she couldn't control her gasp of awareness.

'Clare. Sweet Clare.' He had moved swiftly back to her lips, putting his hands on either side of her head, and was kissing her with increasing passion, taking full advantage of her open mouth to explore, to send her senses whirling.

She made a small sound of protest, tried to make her mind dominate her body and her senses, but then he pulled her against him, his hand low on her hips, and she felt a great surge of hunger deep inside her. With a moan Clare relaxed, Jack giving a cry of triumph against her mouth as he felt it. His own need for her grew into a blaze. His breath was hot, panting, but he was saying her name with joy; he was even laughing with it as he went on kissing her mouth, her throat, her eyes. 'I knew you weren't immune to me; I knew it! That night we spent together was so good. Don't you remember, Clare? Don't you remember how good it was?'

He had parted the front of her blouse and was kissing the deep V between her breasts. Clare's head was thrown back, and her mouth was open on a sigh of sensuous pleasure. 'Yes, I remember,' she said softly.

Lifting his head to look at her, Jack thought that he had never seen anyone so beautiful, so alluring. With her dark hair a dishevelled cloud, and her features softened by open sexual arousal, she enraptured his heart, his body, his senses. He found that he wanted her more than any woman he had ever known, more even than his wife when he had been so young. But this, somehow, was a different kind of need. Overwhelming as it was, there was no arrogance about it. Instead he felt a great humility, like a worshipper at a temple, like a pagan before a goddess. His hands shaking uncontrollably, he could hardly undo the buttons that would reveal her breasts to him, and gave an angry groan of impatience at his own clumsiness until they were free at last and he could feast his eyes on her.

'You're beautiful,' he said hoarsely. 'Even more beautiful.'

He bent to kiss her and she let him, putting her hands on either side of his head, her body moving in voluptuous pleasure, her breath coming in small, almost anguished gasps. Clare opened her eyes a little, the pleasure almost more than she could bear. There was a mirror on the door of the wardrobe, a large full-length mirror. She saw their bodies reflected in it, saw the way she was enjoying his lovemaking. *Jack's* lovemaking. Suddenly she was filled with consternation and dismay. With an appalled exclamation she pushed him away. 'No! Leave me alone.'

Caught off balance, Jack staggered back a couple of steps, completely taken by surprise. For a moment he could only stare, but then his face filled with anger as he saw her hastily cover herself. 'Why?' he demanded harshly.

'I—I don't want this. I don't want you!'

'So what was it, then? A tease? A punishment?'

'You started it!'

'But you weren't exactly fighting me off,' Jack pointed out ruthlessly. 'You wanted it as much as I did.'

'No! Never! How dare you think that you can win me over with a few tawdry caresses?'

Jack's face whitened. 'So why go along with it, then?' He caught her wrist, pulled her round to face him when she would have turned away. 'Did you do it as some sort of cheap revenge on me for wanting to see Toby. Is that it?'

'No. Don't be ridiculous. And take your hand off

me or I'll scream.' Her voice had risen, and there were flushes of colour in her cheeks.

Jack studied her face for a moment, then said sardonically, 'What's the matter, Clare? Are you angry with yourself for forgetting to hate me? Did your body take over and shut everything else out of your mind?'

She jerked her hand away. 'Wasn't it supposed to? Wasn't that why you did it? You're very clever, Jack. Very experienced with women. You told me that sob story about your marriage and knew I'd feel sorry for you. You used it to take advantage of me, to—'

She broke off as Jack, his eyes filling with fury, grabbed her again. 'Damn you, I don't want your pity.' He shook her, saying, 'You little bitch! You're just the same as the rest. Playing with a man's emotions as if it was all a game. First hot then cold. Women don't know how to love. I thought you were different, but you're not. Well, all right. You wanted revenge and now you've got it.'

Clare stared at him, seeing the pain in his eyes. Gropingly she said, 'Jack, I... What are you trying to say?'

'Say? Nothing!' He pushed her towards the door. 'You wanted to leave, so go. Get the hell out of here. Go to your cold-blooded marriage with Paul Venton!'

Turning away, he pulled off his tie and flung it on a chair, then strode into the bathroom and slammed the door.

Clare gazed at the closed door, feeling dazed, unable to take in the swift play of emotions he had shown—his anger, his hurt. Automatically she searched for her bag, her coat, but then stood still as she went to put it on, her eyes going again to the door.

He had accused her of being like his wife—a woman who had no heart, who had treated him so cruelly. But she wasn't like that—was she? She hadn't deliberately encouraged him just to deny him, to throw it back in his face.

She heard the sound of the shower coming on, and remembered Jack's tremulous excitement when he had touched her, her own aching need and the pleasure at his touch. A great shiver ran through her, and she moaned softly. But she hated him. That was quite, quite definite. So why, then, did her body love what he had done to her, why did his touch set her senses on fire, make her crave for more? And only *his* touch, only his.

Jack stood under the shower, unmoving, just letting the water cascade over him. He had never felt so defeated, so bitter. For a few, wonderful minutes he had thought that his life had come good at last. He had seen a future that was golden instead of bleak. But now he was just glad that there had been no opportunity to tell Clare how he felt—at least he had been saved that final humiliation. He knew that he had given her cause to hate him, but he had thought her too warm and generous-hearted not to change, that she would have the courage to admit to her own feelings. But he had been wrong. Completely wrong.

So maybe she did still hate him. Maybe he had been wrong about that, too. But if so why had she let him kiss her, caress her? She had been hotly aroused. It had been no sham; he knew that. But something had got to her. Was it because she was engaged to that wimp, Venton?

A picture of Clare and Venton together came into his mind, not for the first time, and he was suddenly filled with a black rage of jealousy. He slammed his fist against the wall, making the cubicle rattle, and it was then that he heard a faint noise behind him. But, before he could turn, two unsteady hands circled his waist and then held him. He could feel Clare against him—her face against his back, her breasts sensuously soft on his skin, her hips against his thighs and her legs touching his. He gave a great cry and would have turned, but she held him still.

'The soap?' she whispered in his ear.

He found it, gave it to her, and she started to wash his back. She did so slowly, taking her time, while Jack stood very still, almost unable to believe that the unbelievable was happening. Clare finished his back to her satisfaction and her hands moved down, soft, caressing, making him tremble with awareness. Her touch was so delicate, so light and so tantalising! Tremor after tremor ran through him and he made no attempt to hide it; already his breath was hot, uneven, and he knew that he was almost beyond control.

At last, *at last,* she turned him to face her. Her dark hair was drawn back and plastered against her head like a sleek helmet. There were tiny drops of water on her eyelashes, but she blinked them away. She was naked and very lovely. She reached up to wash his chest, but first Jack held her a little away from him so that he could look at her properly, look his fill. Then his eyes came up to meet hers, found them watching him with an uncertain, tentative smile. Leaning forward, he found her mouth and kissed her with long, lingering gentleness, the water splashing off them. When he opened his eyes, Clare was smiling fully. Then she went on washing him.

He was unable to hold out for very long. When she finished his chest and moved down, he could withstand the agonising hunger no longer. Picking her up, he was out of the bathroom and into the bedroom so fast that she hardly knew what was happening. And then he dropped her on the bed, soaking wet as she was. For a moment he knelt over her, his face sharp with desire, small rivulets of water running from his hair down his chest. Clare looked at him, then she smiled and reached out for him.

They needed each other so badly. Their lovemaking was deeply passionate, tempestuous. Selfish at first, as hunger took over they each reached an uncontrollable climax—Jack first, his hoarse, panting groans of excitement echoing her own cries of pleasure, then Clare, travelling along a great, whirling tunnel of delight into an explosion of golden rapture that seemed to last for ever.

Afterwards, still filled with the wonder of it, his heart a giant hammer in his chest, Jack put his arms round Clare and held her very tight. He lifted himself on one elbow but still held her close against him, as close as he could get. With a shaking hand he smoothed the damp hair from her face. 'Sweetheart. My little love.'

He kissed her with intense gratitude and watched as she slowly opened her eyes. He saw the sated sexuality in their green depths, the Mona Lisa smile that played around her mouth. It was the look of a woman who had been well and truly loved, a look of utter content. He laughed deep in his throat, a masculine

laugh of pride and triumph in his own virility. 'I'm
going to buy your friend a crate of the very best champagne,' he chuckled.

'It was good, huh?'

'It was the best.' He moved a little. 'It *is* the best.'
She gave a long, happy sigh and he said, 'Why did
you change your mind? Why didn't you leave?'

'I just stopped fighting—fighting you, fighting myself.' She smiled again, that smile of utter compla-
cency. 'I don't think I reasoned it out at all. I just
acted instinctively. I simply knew that if I walked
away I would lose the chance for ever and that I
would regret it for the rest of my life. I took my
clothes off without even knowing I was doing it.'

The slightest frown seemed to be gathering in her
eyes, but, before it could, Jack kissed her lids, wiping
it away. 'I'm so glad you did, so infinitely glad,' he
assured her. 'It was what I've been longing for, yearning for.' As he spoke he went on kissing her, her
throat, her neck, the lobes of her ears and finally her
lips. 'I want you again,' he said huskily.

'So soon?' She gave a little gasp. 'Oh, yes, you
do.'

'I've waited a long time for tonight.'

Opening her eyes, Clare studied his face, her eyes
widening at the warmth and tenderness she saw there.
'You care about me,' she said on a note of discovery.

'Oh, yes.' Jack gently ran his hand down her face.
'I care.' His hand ran on, brushing her breasts, and
then they were suddenly making love again. But now
they took their time, finding new ways to delight, exploring, sometimes laughing as Jack teased her when
he found that she couldn't stand to have him run his

fingers down her spine—it was just too erotic. Deliberately they held back, prolonging the anticipation, making the bed an oasis of pleasure, each touch, each kiss a wonderful prelude to their growing hunger. Until somehow, almost without any deliberate movement, their bodies joined at last and they both experienced the most brilliant, mind-blowing excitement they had ever known.

They fell asleep, their bodies still entwined, and it was a couple of hours later that Clare woke, the light, which they'd left on, slowly penetrating her subconscious. She became aware first of the most wonderful peace of mind, a euphoric state of warm happiness that she had seldom in her life known before. Then she moved slightly and felt the tenderness deep inside herself that one gets after passionate lovemaking. There was an emptiness there, too—the emptiness that a lover leaves behind and which can only be filled when he makes love to you again. A not unpleasant sensation at first, but one that can lead to the most terrible frustration if it isn't soon satisfied. Clare had known that frustration of old, and it made her open her eyes now in sudden panic.

She relaxed at once. Jack was still there. He was awake, sitting up in bed watching her, a pensive expression in his grey eyes. But he smiled when he saw that she was awake too. Pushing herself up, Clare leaned against his chest and lifted her face for his kiss. Her hair had dried into a mass of soft curls and she looked very lovely.

'What were you thinking?' she asked. 'You looked very serious.'

'About you, of course.' Her breasts were bare and

he began to stroke them idly, gently toying with them. Clare put up a hand to push her hair off her face and he stopped, then took hold of her hand.

She felt his body tense, and looked down. She was still wearing Paul's ring and it held Jack's gaze, his face hardening. 'Why don't you take that off?' he suggested, keeping his tone even. He went to say something else, but then stopped.

Guessing what it was, Clare took off the ring and put it on the bedside table, then put her hands on his shoulders as she looked into his eyes, holding them. 'I have never been to bed with Paul,' she said earnestly. 'We've never been lovers.'

'I'm very glad to hear it.' His lips twisted. 'Although it confirms my opinion of him. Would you have got engaged to him if I hadn't come on the scene?'

'Probably not,' Clare admitted.

'And now?'

It was a loaded question in the circumstances. She wondered if Jack wasn't yet completely sure of her and it was some kind of test. So she thought for a moment before saying, 'I'll break it off. But I want to do it gently; I don't want to humiliate him. After all, he—' She stopped.

'If you think Venton was doing you a favour, you're completely wrong,' Jack said, anticipating what she'd been going to say. 'He'd do almost anything to get at me.'

'But I was seeing him occasionally before you found out about Toby,' Clare protested.

Jack shrugged. 'Which was a lucky break for him. And I'll say one thing for Paul Venton—he'll always take full advantage of any break that comes his way, whether by fair means or not. I bet he was around a lot more once our involvement became public knowledge.'

Which was true, Clare realised. Her eyes drew into a troubled frown but, seeing it, Jack kissed her.

'Forget about Venton,' he murmured. He slid down in the bed and drew her head down to kiss her. 'Make love to me,' he commanded.

Clare pretended to be affronted. 'Oh, so we're giving orders now, are we?'

'Please,' he said in mock humility. 'Pretty, pretty please.'

She said, 'That's better,' in a severe tone, then spoilt it all by giggling as she happily obeyed him.

They left the hotel separately—Jack a couple of hours before Clare, as he was flying out to Northern Canada that morning to be present at the start of an attempt by a team of women to walk to the North Pole, an event he was sponsoring. Using the car phone, she checked that Toby was OK, then called Paul and asked him to meet her at her flat.

She got held up in heavy traffic so he arrived first and was sitting in the back of his car, using it as a mobile office while he waited. Clare got out of her own car, not looking forward to the next half-hour one little bit.

'You'll have to give me a key,' Paul remarked. Once they were inside the lobby he kissed her, then said, 'You look different.' Clare flushed, wondering if it was so obvious that she'd spent a night in Jack's arms. But then he added, 'You've done your hair in a new style.'

'It got wet,' she explained.

'What happened last night?' he asked, when they were in her flat.

'Last night?'

'You said a friend was in a fix. That was why you broke our date, wasn't it?'

'Yes.' She made a dismissive gesture, her face becoming serious. 'Paul, I'm very sorry. There's no easy way to say this. But I no longer want to go on with our—our arrangement. I want to break off the engagement.'

She saw him stiffen, his face become set, and for a moment he didn't speak, the silence becoming charged with tension.

'I see. And may I ask why?' he demanded caustically.

'Things have changed. I've—I've seen Jack. Talked to him. And I've decided to let him have as much access to Toby as they both want.'

Paul's face sharpened. 'What happened to make you change your mind?'

'That's—private. I'm sorry,' she repeated.

'So you damn well ought to be,' he said angrily. 'Do you realise what a laughing stock this is going to make me? Getting engaged one month and having it broken off the next! Have you met someone new? Is that it?'

'No.'

'But there must be someone; you wouldn't have changed your mind otherwise.' His eyes narrowed. 'So if it isn't someone new...' He paused, and then said on a note of discovery, 'So maybe it's someone old. Yes, that's it! My God, you're going back to Jack Straker. Even after everything you've said about him—how you hated him, didn't want him near Toby.' He gave an angry, derisive laugh. 'Well, thank you very much, Clare.'

Not attempting to deny it, Clare said, 'It just happened. I didn't want it, look for it. I suppose it was just always there.'

'Hate isn't far removed from love, is that what you're saying? Or in this case lust,' he sneered.

Clare's face tightened. 'I realise that you must be angry, Paul, but—'

'Yes, I am angry. Damn angry!' Striding to her, he took hold of her arm. 'I suppose you were with Straker last night?' He saw by her face that he was right and, his voice rising furiously, he said, 'You realise you've behaved like a cheap slut?' His fist bunched and he raised it threateningly. 'But then that's what you are. Nothing but a dirty—'

'You having trouble, Clare?'

The voice startled them both. They swung round to stare at the tall, handsome man who strolled out of the bedroom. At least he had some clothes on this time.

'Sean,' Clare gasped, and felt a surge of relief. Pulling herself away from Paul, she said, 'Please leave.'

Recovering from his stunned surprise, and having recognised Sean, Paul gave a contemptuous laugh. 'It seems you have men crawling out of the woodwork. But what more could you expect from—'

'The lady told you to leave.' Sean flexed muscles

that women drooled over. 'And it would give me great pleasure to throw you down the stairs.'

Paul made quite a dignified exit in the circumstances, drawing himself up and marching to the door, even if rather hurriedly. There he turned and said curtly, 'You'll regret this.'

When he'd gone, Clare sagged with relief. 'Lord, I'm glad you were here. Thanks. He was starting to get a bit nasty.'

'So I gathered.' Sean slumped in an armchair, his legs stretched out and seeming to take up half the space in the room. 'I thought I'd stay out of sight until he'd gone, but when I heard him shouting I figured you could use some help.'

'You were right. But what are you doing here?'

He looked somewhat shamefaced. 'Well, we knew you and Toby were going to be away for the night, so...' He opened his hands eloquently. 'Tanya slipped away early, but I guess I must have overslept. I was just about to leave when you showed up.'

Clare went to the window and saw that Paul's car was still outside, and she thought he was sitting inside it. 'He hasn't gone yet,' she said uneasily.

'Then I'll wait till he does, just in case he's hanging around to have another go at you,' Sean offered.

'That's very kind of you. I could do with a coffee; how about you?'

They chatted for a while, Clare going several times to look out of the window, but it was another twenty minutes before she saw Paul's car eventually pull away.

'He's gone,' she said with satisfaction.

'I'd better get along, too. They were doing some

script changes this morning, but we're shooting again this afternoon.'

'And I must go to work.'

They left together, chatting about Tanya as they went down in the lift and through the lobby, Sean with a casual hand on her shoulder. The caretaker opened the door for them, they stepped outside—and were immediately assaulted by a barrage of flashing cameras.

'Hell!' Sean exclaimed. He reached for his dark glasses, but it was far too late to try and hide his identity. There must have been half a dozen cameramen and reporters, all eagerly crowding round, shouting questions at them. They pushed their way through, and Sean saw her to her car, then hesitated. 'I was going to get a cab, but...'

'I'll give you a lift,' Clare offered, desperate to escape the flashes that were going off in her face.

They raced away, and Sean cursed angrily. 'That guy you threw out must have arranged this. He must have called the papers the minute he left your apartment and waited outside to make sure they arrived.

'Paul did it? Oh, no!'

'Hey, it's no big deal. Tanya will know the truth.'

Clare didn't find that of much comfort, but supposed that it would soon blow over. She dropped Sean off in the West End and went to work.

She was wrong about it blowing over. There must have been a dearth of news that week, because not only the next morning but for days afterwards the papers held the story. The headlines on the tabloids stated categorically that she and Sean were lovers.

SUPERSTAR'S LONDON LOVE NEST, one read. It also listed the number of times that Sean had been seen entering or leaving the building. Where on earth they'd got that information from Clare had no idea, unless it was from the caretaker of her building. The fact that she had been involved with Jack led to another headline: TYCOON LOSES OUT TO SEAN MUNRO.

Of her engagement to Paul the papers said surprisingly little—just that he had broken off the engagement as soon as he'd become aware that she was having an affair with Sean. Which made Paul come out of the whole thing smelling of roses, even though it had been he who had given the false information to the press. Clare got really indignant about that, and wanted to sue him or something.

She called Sean, having to do so from an anonymous hotel phone because she couldn't be sure that someone wasn't listening in to her own phone or the mobile. He rather tersely told her not to make a fuss. 'Just let it all die down,' he advised her. 'Try to ignore them. Believe me, it's the only way.'

'But none of it is true! Couldn't I at least get my lawyer to issue a denial?'

'A waste of time,' Sean told her. 'People believe what they want to believe, and any statement you make will only add fuel to the fire.'

'But this is hurting my son. I have to do something.'

'So what would you say?' Sean demanded. 'That I wasn't meeting you? That it was a friend? If you do the press either won't believe you or they'll go all out to find out who the friend is. Which will lead them to Tanya. You promised to keep our secret, Clare.'

'Then isn't it time that you and Tanya made up your minds?' she said rather tartly.

'It's for Tanya to decide,' he told her. 'Look, I have to go; I'm needed on the set.'

After that very dissatisfying conversation, Clare managed to reach Tanya, but her friend refused to talk to her on the phone in case it was bugged. So they met in a restaurant, where Tanya turned up wearing sunglasses even darker than Sean's and with her hair completely hidden by a floppy-brimmed hat.

'Anyone would think it was you who were being hounded by the press,' Clare remarked, with a surprised and not exactly pleased laugh.

'Brian said I wasn't to see you again until all this blows over.'

'Brian said!' Clare exclaimed indignantly. 'Since when did you take any notice of what your husband says?'

'Is it very bad?' Tanya asked—with more curiosity than sympathy, Clare thought.

'Yes, it is. I can't go anywhere without the press following me. They come to the shop, to the flat. They even followed me to a sale I went to. Toby's having a terrible time at school. And the worst of it is that I'm going through it all when I'm not the one involved. I really think that you and Sean must come into the open, Tanya. I can't take much more of this. It was bad enough when they found out about me and Jack, but this is far worse. This—why, it's not much short of persecution.'

Her friend's elegantly manicured fingers fiddled with a bread roll. 'I'm dreadfully sorry for you, of course. But it was your ex-fiancé who told the press.

And Sean is going through it as well. He's hardly
been off the set of the film all week.'

'Have you discussed it?'

'Well, sort of.'

'What's that supposed to mean, Tanya?'

Looking uncomfortable, Tanya said, 'Well, actually, all this publicity and everything—it's put me off
a bit.'

Clare stared. 'You mean, put you off Sean?'

'It's not the kind of thing I'm used to. And my
parents would hate it. And then there are the children
to think of.'

Her face growing grim, Clare said, 'And what
about my child? It's because of you that he's going
through all this.'

'That's hardly fair. I told you right from the start I
couldn't make up my mind.'

'But you thought you'd try Sean out while you
were thinking about it, is that it?' Clare said coldly.
'And to hell with everyone else.'

'I've decided to stay with Brian. I don't want to
argue with you, Clare, but—'

Clare got to her feet, cold with anger. 'You won't
have the chance!' And she strode out of the restaurant.

When she got to her shop she tried to call Jack at
his office, but was told that he was still away, having
gone on to the States from Canada. His secretary refused to give her his private number or the name of
his hotel, which was fair enough, Clare supposed—
but it disturbed her that he hadn't tried to phone her
while he was away. His only recognition of the night
they'd spent together had been a hastily written letter
from the airport, saying how wonderful it had been

and that he would tell her so properly as soon as he got back.

But an enterprising reporter, tipped off by someone at the hotel where she had stayed with Jack, found out that the room had been paid for by Sean, which led to yet another suggestive headline, the fact that Sean hadn't even been there with her being deliberately overlooked. Clare decided that enough was enough, and was only waiting for Jack to get home to corroborate her story before seeing a lawyer. Toby was miserable, too—and, to crown it all, the court actually wrote to her, demanding to know her present circumstances, because Paul had told them that the engagement was off and that he thought her unfit to keep Toby.

Clare seethed with anger over that, and left a message at Jack's office to say that she wanted to see him the minute he returned.

But it was another couple of days before she finally saw him. On the following Friday Jack's secretary rang to say that he was home and he would meet Clare the following morning—his time for seeing Toby—on board HMS Belfast, the warship that was permanently moored in the Thames near the Tower of London. Clare was more than a little surprised that he hadn't phoned himself, or even called at the flat, but could only say that she and Toby would be there.

There was just one reporter hanging around hopefully outside her building. Clare took a taxi whose driver entered into the spirit of the thing and managed to lose him. When they reached the ship Clare looked round eagerly for Jack and saw him sitting on a seat nearby, apparently reading the paper. Toby saw him at the same time and ran over to him. Picking him up, Jack made a big fuss of him, then gave him a model of a Mountie he'd brought back for the boy. Clare watched, the light of happiness and expectation in her face slowly dying as Jack gave all his attention to Toby, hardly even glancing at her. He bought tickets to go aboard, but he didn't speak to her until they were on the deck of the old grey-painted ship and Toby was happily exploring.

'You left a message saying you wanted to see me,' he said, his voice cold.

Clare stared. 'What's the matter? Why are you being like this?' she demanded.

His eyes came up to meet hers. They weren't the eyes of a lover—not even a friend. They were hard, implacable. He might have been her enemy, he was so cold and withdrawn.

'What is it?' she said again, her voice unsteady, failing her. A tightness gripped her throat, her chest, and she knew that he was going to reject her again, that history was about to repeat itself.

'I read the papers,' Jack said harshly. 'I know that you've been having an affair with Sean Munro.' He turned away, unable to look at her, and went to stand at the ship's rail, gripping it with white-knuckled hands.

He hadn't even wanted to see her today, but he knew it had to be faced. And it was best to get the whole damn business over and done with. Toby came up and he spoke to him, but in his mind he was bitterly remembering how reluctantly he had left her that day to keep his appointment in Canada. She had looked so damned sexy, lying there in the bed, that he'd wanted her yet again and had had to drag himself away. But there had been the promise of a future together, the three of them, and he had been full of happiness as he'd left, eager to get his business over, to get back to her.

But then, only twenty-four hours later, he had picked up a copy of an English paper and seen Clare's photograph along with that of Sean Munro splashed across the front page. The story had been carried over to the inside page, and there he'd found his own picture, his own involvement in the sordid mess. At first he'd been incredulous, unable to believe it. He'd waited for Clare or Munro to issue a denial, but none had come.

Then had come the statement from Paul Venton, saying that he'd broken his engagement because he'd found out about the affair. Venton, Jack knew, was the proverbial rat that would lead the rest off the sinking ship. But he tended to guard his dignity, and it had seemed strange that he had said anything at all in the circumstances. He must have been feeling very vindictive to make a statement like that.

A dozen times Jack had picked up the phone to call Clare but had changed his mind. He'd been told that she had phoned his office, but even then he hadn't contacted her, still waiting for the denial that didn't appear. Instead a veritable list of the number of times Munro had visited the flat had been printed in one of the more probing tabloids. It had claimed that several people who lived and worked in the building had seen and recognised him; they had seen him let himself into Clare's flat with a key. One or two of them had even been willing to give their names and have their simpering photographs appear. In a rage of anger Jack had thrown down the paper.

It was all there. All that was missing were the denials and threats of lawsuits that innocent people would have made. So what the hell was he supposed to think?

Her voice sounding unnatural even to her own ears, Clare said, 'And did you believe it?'

Turning, he looked at her face. 'Do you deny it?'

There was a taut silence until Clare broke it with a harsh laugh. 'You did! You did believe it. Some gutter paper prints a story they've dredged up from a chance meeting and a whole load of lies told them out of spite and resentment, and you believe every damn word of it! You don't even bother to phone me and ask if it's true. You just naturally go ahead and think the worst of me.'

'So I'm asking you now—is it true?'

But Clare was filled with overwhelming anger and bitterness, and only said malevolently, 'So much for saying you cared! I wish to hell I'd walked out of that room, that I'd never gone to bed with you. And I—' She broke off abruptly as some people came in sight, looking at them curiously as they heard her raised voice.

Her face flushed with emotion, she swung away and walked to the stern of the ship, stood looking unseeingly at the panorama of the river spread out before her. Her hair was loose and the breeze caught it, blowing it about her head. She lifted a hand to push it off her face and took advantage of it to wipe away a tear. She wouldn't let him see her cry; she wouldn't!

Jack came up behind her. 'So tell me,' he said urgently, hoping against hope.

But Clare was fighting a battle to hide her broken heart, and she brought out the big guns. Rounding on him, the light of hatred back in her eyes, she said in a voice of clear bitterness, 'Yes, of course it's true. Sean came to my flat all those times. Yes, he had a key to let himself in. And yes—' her voice grew contemptuous '—I went straight from your bed to the flat to meet Sean. I'm sure your nasty little mind will know what interpretation to put on that!'

Jack's face had whitened, grown tense. He made to reach out for her, then shoved his fists in his pockets. 'Are you saying that—'

'Yes!' Clare's voice was the snarl of a wounded animal fighting back. 'I'm saying anything you want to believe.' He stared at her, completely lost for words, and she tossed her head and laughed again. 'I'm sure you and Toby can manage without me.' And she strode past him, walking with head held high until she was out of sight. She slumped then, leaning against one of the gun turrets, her eyes squeezed tightly shut in raw hurt. But then she pulled herself together and went on, went home.

Jack brought Toby home a few hours later. Clare unlocked the front door at his ring, but he didn't ask to come up so she didn't see him. Toby was full of his visit and she tried hard to join in his enthusiasm, but she was pleased when he sat down to draw a picture of the ship for Jack. He must be getting quite a picture gallery by now, Clare thought despondently. She sat in a chair, watching her son. He looked so like Jack, a constant reminder of what might have been. If Jack had trusted her, if he had really cared.

Tears ran silently down her face and she let them run, merely turning her head so that Toby wouldn't see. Bleakly she wondered if Jack would use her 'confession' to try and take the boy away from her—say she was unfit to bring him up. Probably. The way her life was going at the moment she was quite prepared to believe it could happen, believe that Jack would be that cruel.

Maybe that was why he wanted to believe that she'd had an affair with Sean, she thought dully. He desperately wanted Toby. Was that the reason he'd gone to bed with her? Had he been willing to marry her to get him? But now, this way, he could see a chance of getting Toby without having to have her along as well. The pain of it all went very deep.

What especially hurt was that she had been happy for so little time. In going to bed with Jack she had at last admitted to herself what had always been there in her heart—that, ever since that first time, when her son had been conceived, she had been head over heels in love with him. It was why no other man had even attracted her over the years. She had told herself she was fastidious, but it hadn't been that. It had been a basic love for one man that nothing could replace. And now he had thrown it back in her face yet again.

She had been due to go out to dinner that evening with some friends of her late parents—respectable people who kept in touch with her for their sakes—but the husband had phoned earlier in the week to tell her that his wife was ill and that they'd have to cancel the dinner. Clare didn't believe him; she knew it was the scandal in the papers. She supposed she could expect her respectable friends to drop her, and the more salacious, who wanted to hear the whole story, to want to see her. Already there had been several invitations left on the answer machine. Her work, too, was being affected—a couple of clients had cancelled commissions.

But the biggest worry was how it would affect Toby. He must, as always, come before everything else. Clare realised that she had come to yet another crisis in her life, and she had to decide whether to sit and wait it all out, try and go on as before—or whether to run, sell up everything here and go abroad to live, start again where she wouldn't be known. Australia or some place like that.

Getting up, she went to look out of the window. It would be a terrible wrench to leave. She loved London, loved Britain. The tears fell more freely but she still stood stiffly in front of the window, not letting her son see that her life had been shattered yet again.

CHAPTER NINE

A WEEK later Jack, too, stood at a window, gazing into space. But then he seemed to have spent most of the past seven days being unable to concentrate on work or anything else. The story had at last disappeared from the papers, but everyone would have seen it. His lawyer had even called to ask him if he now wanted to apply for custody of Toby, to say that they would have a good chance of it being granted. Jack had said that he'd think about it; he'd call him back.

And he had thought of little else, sitting pensively at his desk or in a chair in front of a blank television screen at home. There had been a charity première of a film that he'd attended, but afterwards he hadn't been able to remember any of the story. He hadn't returned the lawyer's call; he still hadn't made up his mind.

He realised that it was raining heavily, and roused himself; it was time to go and collect Toby. He'd intended taking him out somewhere, but the weather had put paid to that. There was always a museum, Jack supposed, but then gave a grimace and decided to bring the boy back here. Fleetingly he wondered if Clare would come too, how he would feel and act if she did. But he knew at once that she wouldn't; she would rather leave him alone with Toby than see him again.

The boy was waiting for Jack in the lobby of the

apartment building. He seemed subdued, and sat quietly in the back of the car, but brightened up when they stopped at a toy shop and he chose a model aeroplane to make up. Jack got him settled in the kitchen, spreading an old newspaper on the work surface, and helping him with the model when it proved too difficult for his small fingers. They talked, and Toby sang a song for him that he'd learned at school, which enchanted Jack. Quite a lot of glue and paint got spilt, but Toby was thrilled with his finished model. He ran round the flat with it held in his outstretched arm, making jet-plane noises.

Jack laughed and glanced at his watch; only just time to take Toby for some lunch before he had to take him home. He stripped off the top few layers of newspaper, the ones that were sticky with glue, and dropped them in the bin, turned to clear up the rest. Toby had come over and was looking at the paper. He pointed to a picture of a man, and Jack saw with a tremendous feeling of guilt that it was Sean Munro.

'That's the man who was in the space film,' he told Jack. 'He gave me his auto—auto...' He struggled, but couldn't remember the word. 'I've got a poster of the film up on the wall in my room,' he explained to Jack. 'He wrote his name on it. And he put, "To Toby, a fellow space traveller". I know because Auntie Tanya read it out to me.'

'Auntie Tanya?' Jack queried, thinking more about gathering up the paper and getting it out of Toby's sight. 'Who's she?'

'She's the man's friend. She was at home with him one day when Jonesy brought me home from school.'

Jack grew very still, the paper half crumpled in his

hands. 'Was your mother there?' he asked, trying to keep his tone even.

'No, she was at work. There was only Auntie Tanya and the Spacefleet Commander,' Toby said, giving Sean his title in the film. 'They were just going, so it was lucky we got a lift home or we wouldn't have seen him and he wouldn't have signed my poster.'

'Is Auntie Tanya your mother's sister?' Jack asked rather hoarsely.

'No, she's Mummy's friend. Her other name is Mrs Beresford. And she's got a boy and a girl. But they don't go to my school, though we sometimes all go to the park together to play.' Toby explained it patiently, his eyes bright and intelligent. But then they clouded. 'Only Mummy doesn't take me to the park much now. There are horrid men who keep following us.' He looked at Jack hopefully. 'If you came with us they might not chase us.'

Jack was staring at him, his thoughts racing. Had he been wrong? Had they all been wrong—the press, the gossips? And Paul Venton, too? Oh, God, he hoped so; *he hoped so*. Unsteadily he said, 'Let's go and get some lunch.'

They went to Toby's favourite hamburger place and, although Jack bought something for himself as well, he couldn't eat; he just sat there in growing excitement and hope. If Clare was innocent then it explained her extreme anger. And if she was safeguarding the reputation of a married friend, then it also gave a reason for the lack of denials. He had to see her, talk to her. Impatient now, he waited for Toby to finish his meal then drove him home.

Clare unlocked the front entrance door and Jack

came inside with Toby, then took him up in the lift. Clare was waiting at the door of the flat, her face paling when she saw Jack. 'I have to talk to you,' he said forcibly, and stuck his foot in the door so she couldn't slam it shut on him.

'I have nothing to say to you. Will you please go away?'

'No—not until I've talked to you.'

She tried to push him out, but he shouldered his way in. When he looked at her face it caught at his heart; there were dark shadows of sleeplessness round her eyes, and she looked pale and drawn.

'Look what I made.' Toby proudly showed off his model.

'That's terrific.' Clare squatted down to take a closer look. Her heart was thumping at seeing Jack, but she knew that this visit could only mean that he intended to try to take Toby from her. He probably thought that she was some kind of nymphomaniac and had come to check on whether she had a man here or not, Clare imagined bitterly. She admired the plane a little longer, then took off Toby's jacket. 'Hey, what's this on your shirt? Paint? Maybe it would be a good idea if you changed it.'

She sent him out to his bedroom, then rose to face Jack, trying not to let him see how vulnerable she was, trying to avoid his eyes. Expecting him to tell her that he was going to try for custody of Toby, she said coldly, 'All right. Say it.'

Jack had been watching her with the boy, his heart warmed by the obvious love between them, a love he so much wanted to share, be part of. He knew he was playing for high stakes, that he had everything to lose.

Perhaps it shouldn't have mattered that she'd been having an affair with another man, but it did, it hurt like the constant cut of a sharp saw, tearing at his heart.

Strangely he knew that it wouldn't have mattered quite so much if it had been Venton she'd been having an affair with; Venton was a wimp who didn't count. But Sean Munro came across as a man, a force to be reckoned with, and Jack recognised that a great part of his agony of mind was from pure and utter jealousy. He didn't want Clare to have been to bed with anyone else—he wanted her for himself and his imagination wouldn't let it alone. He pictured her making love with Sean Munro and could hardly contain his despair and anger. He had to know whether or not she'd been to bed with the damn man, *he had to*!

Desperate to find out, Jack decided to try to surprise the truth out of her. So, without preamble, he demanded, 'Why didn't you tell me it was your friend Tanya Beresford who was having the affair with Munro?'

Clare gasped, the question so completely different from what she'd expected, and blurted out, 'How did you find out?' In bewilderment, she could only think of one way, and said, 'Did she—did she tell you herself?'

Jack's eyes grew warm, and his voice softened in profound relief as he said, 'No, it seems your friend isn't as concerned for you as you are for her. It was Toby who told me.' He took hold of her arm. 'Come and look.' Leading her into Toby's room, where the boy was finding a space on his bedside table for the plane, Jack pointed to the poster on the wall. There was the autograph, scrawled in Sean's hand. A small gesture for a little boy, but one that Jack hoped was going to make all the difference in the world to their lives.

When she'd read it, Jack drew Clare back into the sitting-room. 'Toby and Jonesy came home early one afternoon,' he explained. 'They found the two of them here and Toby recognised Sean from the film.'

Clare shook her head in wonder. 'I didn't even notice.'

'Did you lend them your flat to meet in? Is that what happened?'

Reluctantly she nodded. 'I wish I hadn't now.'

'So why did you?'

She shrugged. 'Tanya was pretty desperate. She couldn't make up her mind what to do. I thought that if it was made easy for her, became a commonplace, then it might not seem so exciting and she'd go back to Brian. Her husband,' she explained. She gave a short laugh. 'It worked, too, although not in the way I intended. She has gone back to her husband.'

'You mean she turned down Sean Munro?'

'Oh, no, she fancied Sean. What she turned down was all the publicity that surrounded him: being hounded by newspaper reporters, the constant demands for an interview, the flashguns going off in your face, the complete invasion of privacy for you and your family,' Clare said bitterly. 'She left all that to me.'

'So why didn't you deny it to the papers?'

With an exasperated sigh, Clare said, 'I wanted to, but if I had I would also have had to break my promise to Tanya. Brian would have found out and it would have ruined her marriage; there would have been no husband to go back to. And she has children,' she added feelingly.

'So you took it all on your own shoulders.'

Something in his voice made her glance at him, and Clare saw the light of hope and tenderness in his eyes. She stood still, staring. Jack moved to go to her, take her in his arms, but Clare held him off, her face filling with antagonism. 'Don't you dare touch me!'

'But don't you see? This changes everything.'

With a contemptuous laugh, Clare said, 'Oh, I see. You think that because you've found out the truth then everything's OK again—we can go back to where we were before. Is that it?' Her face sharpened. 'You arrogant bastard! You've kicked me out of your life twice, and if you think I want anything more to do with you then you're crazy!'

'If you remember, I did ask you if it was true and you not only didn't deny it, you let me believe it,' Jack pointed out. His voice was mild; he wasn't in the least disconcerted by her anger because he was supremely confident, filled with a tremendous exultation. He knew she was his. He had only to let her anger expend itself, let her get it out of her system, and then he would kiss her, coax her, make her admit that she loved him.

But his cool assumption that she would just fall into his arms infuriated Clare. 'If you'd really cared about me—'

'I do care about you,' Jack interrupted. 'That's why it damn well hurt so much.'

His words registered, but Clare ignored them. Going on as if he hadn't spoken, she said, 'If you'd really cared you would have trusted me. You wouldn't have let the rumours, the lies, make any difference.'

'Do you think I wanted to believe them? I daily expected you to issue a denial—but there was nothing, just more evidence to give weight to the rumours. I thought it was possible you'd been having an affair with him. I wanted desperately to hope that it was over, that the night we spent together meant something.'

Clare stared at him for a moment, then laughed aloud. 'My God, did you think it was *you* that had been rejected? Well, good; I'm glad you did. Now you know what it feels like. And you can go on feeling it.'

'If I hurt you all those years ago as much as I've been hurting this past week, then I infinitely regret it. But at least it tells me one thing—that you must have cared for me a very great deal.' He held her gaze steadily. 'And I think that you still care, despite what's happened. I hoped we had a future together. I still hope that.'

'"A future together"!' Clare gave an astonished laugh, her voice rising. 'You must be out of your mind. There's no way I'd even want you to touch me ever again, let alone anything more.'

'I don't believe that. You're as miserable about it as I am. And as for touching you...'

He went to reach for her again, but Clare hoisted her skirt and raised a long, shapely leg to kick out at him. 'Get away from me, you rat!' she yelled at him.

'You wildcat! Ouch!' She caught him on the shin and he jumped back, holding her at arm's length so that she couldn't reach him. But Clare continued to kick out at him, and neither of them noticed the door to the hall open and Toby look in.

'You chauvinist pig!' she shouted at him. 'You're the last man I'd want to live with. I'd rather go to bed with a dozen Sean Munros than you.'

'How many Paul Ventons?' Jack asked.

'Thousands of them.'

'Hey!' he exclaimed when she gave a high kick that any girl in a can-can line would have been proud of. 'You fight dirty. You could have ruined my matrimonial prospects just then.' He began to laugh. 'And I'm rather hoping that my matrimonial prospects are of some considerable interest to you.'

'Marry you? You must be mad! I wouldn't marry you even if you ever got round to telling me you loved me.'

By now Jack was laughing uncontrollably. 'Well, I might if you ever stop kicking me long enough.' He did a swift sidestep and pulled her off balance. 'Come here, you witch.' He caught her in his arms. 'You beautiful, adorable idiot. You know darn well I'm crazy about you.'

For a moment she held herself stiffly, gazing into his eyes, but she saw there all the tenderness and love she had ever hoped for, ever yearned for through all the long, empty years. She relaxed and began to smile, but then the sound of a door slamming reached her ears and she turned her head towards the sound. 'What was that?'

'Just a door somewhere.' Jack, oblivious to everything else, began to draw her towards him.

'It sounded like our front door.' Suddenly she was

uneasy. 'Toby.' Pushing herself free, Clare ran to the window. 'Look in his room.'

Jack hesitated for only a moment, then ran to obey her. Within a couple of minutes he was back. 'He's not there. I can't find him,' he said tersely, just as Clare gave an exclamation of dismay as she saw her son run out of the building.

'Oh, no! He must have seen us fighting.' She ran for the door, with Jack close behind her. Not waiting for the lift, they pelted down the stairs and out of the entrance. Clare ran through the gates and turned to the right.

'Where will he go?' Jack demanded, pounding along beside her.

'To Jonesy. To the hostel.'

It was still pouring with rain, and their flying feet splashed through puddles as they ran. Clare hadn't waited to put on a coat, and Jack was wearing only his suit. Soon their clothes were soaked and their hair was plastered to their heads, making Clare push it impatiently out of her eyes. It was Saturday afternoon and there was a big football match in the area that day. The road was packed with cars and coaches and the pavements thronged with people, mostly men queuing for buses or walking to the ground. They had to dodge round them, Clare desperately trying to look for Toby.

'Can you see him?' she asked anxiously.

'No.' Jack knocked against a woman with a shopping bag, called out an apology and ran on.

'He'll have to cross two roads to get to the hostel. And there's all this traffic,' Clare said in distress.

'Don't worry, we'll catch him up.' Jack took her hand, and gripped it tightly for a moment.

They came to the first road and went to cross, but the lights changed and the traffic came rushing across—the usual London rat-race with every car for itself and to hell with the other traffic, and especially the everlasting nuisance of pedestrians.

Jack grabbed Clare and pulled her back, his eyes sweeping the opposite side of the road. 'Look! There he is.' He pointed to a momentary gap in the hurrying football fans, and Clare just caught a glimpse of Toby running along and about to turn down another street.

'Oh, hurry up! Hurry up and change,' Clare pleaded to the traffic lights, her heart consumed by anxiety.

The lights changed to red at last, and they were across the road, had turned the corner and were tearing along. Here there weren't so many people, and they were able to make better time. They could see Toby ahead of them, and gradually began to gain. He didn't look round and seemed unaware of them behind him. They were catching him up fast, Jack several yards in front, when he reached the next street to be crossed. The lights were still green but the road was momentarily clear. Without waiting, Toby began to run across.

'Toby!' They both yelled his name together, their voices raised in alarm. He checked, looked round. And it was at that moment that a van came fast round the corner, trying to beat the lights before they changed.

Clare screamed with anguished terror as she saw Toby freeze. But it was Jack who seemed to fly across the road, pick Toby up from almost under the van's wheels and throw him out of the way. Then the heavy van hit Jack. For an agonising moment it seemed that he would go under the wheels but then he seemed to bounce off the bonnet, and was thrown onto the pavement, all arms and legs, like a rag doll.

Somehow Clare got across the road, grabbed Toby, who was wailing in terror, and bent over Jack. He was unconscious, but she couldn't see any blood and didn't know if that was a good sign or bad. With shaking hands, her breath sobbing in her throat, she tried to pat his face. 'Jack. Oh, please, Jack, wake up. Wake up.'

The van driver got out and ran over to them. 'He ran out in front of me! I couldn't stop.'

'Get an ambulance,' Clare screamed at him.

She held Toby against her with one arm, hiding his face in her shoulder. With the other she felt for Jack's pulse, but couldn't feel it because her hand was trembling so much. From nowhere a crowd began to gather. Someone had a mobile phone. 'They're coming,' she was told. 'The ambulance will be here in minutes.'

But to Clare they seemed the longest minutes in the world, each moment taking an hour, a lifetime. She cradled Jack's head with her hands, kept calling his name, but his eyes stayed shut. An ambulance had been on its way to the football ground but had been diverted, and was there within a very short time. The paramedics ministered to Jack efficiently, but beyond saying, 'He's alive,' they told her little else. She and Toby climbed into the ambulance with him, and she sat with the boy on her lap, trying to keep out of the way, watching Jack with anxious terror as they drove fast to the nearest hospital.

Clare had no money with her, but someone gave them a hot drink and a towel to dry their hair. Toby had stopped crying, but clung to her very tightly. Clare comforted him as best she could, tried to tell him that everything would be all right, but she was so worried for Jack that she could think of little else. A rather harassed young nurse at last came to tell her that Jack had regained consciousness but was being taken for an X-ray. They went on waiting, for over another hour. Toby fell asleep on Clare's lap, and their clothes dried on them in the warm, stuffy atmosphere.

Picturing Jack with at least a fractured skull, Clare had got to the stage where she felt that she would start screaming if someone didn't tell her how he was, tell her *something* soon, when a nurse came into the waiting area, leading Jack towards them. He was actually walking! And there was even a rueful smile on his lips as the girl, knowing he was a celebrity and excited by it, fussed over him. Clare stared—then burst into tears.

'Hey, now.' He sat down beside her. 'Tears—for me?'

'Oh, God, I thought you were dead or terribly injured.'

'I am terribly injured. Look.' Pushing aside his jacket, he showed her his arm, which was in a plaster cast and held in a sling. 'My wrist is broken. I shall need tender loving care for weeks.'

She gazed into his face for a long moment, then gave a small smile. 'Weeks?'

'Probably months.' He bent forward to kiss her. 'Possibly even years.' He kissed her again. 'The whole of my life, even.'

'Did you get a bump on the head?'

'Why?'

Clare reached up to stroke his face. 'You may not know what you're saying.'

'What I'm saying is that I love you very much, my darling, and that I want you to marry me.'

Clare looked at him, her eyes soft, smiling. 'Oh? When?'

'Tomorrow, if not sooner.'

She laughed, pretended to hesitate. 'I shall have to ask my son.' She glanced at Toby, who had woken and was staring at them. 'Well, Toby? What do you think?'

He looked at them both for a minute, then smiled and, kneeling up on Clare's lap, reached up to put his arms round both their necks, giving them a hug so tight he nearly strangled them. When he let them go Clare, misty eyed, said, 'I think that's ''yes'', for both of us.'

Jack grinned, glanced round at the shabby waiting-room with its rows of chairs, the people waiting, the smell of damp clothes, then grimaced. 'Lord, what a place to propose!'

Clare put her hand over his and looked at him with open love in her eyes. 'I wouldn't have it any other way.'

Jack's heart swelled; he felt that it was too big for his chest. After a moment he got to his feet, and said huskily, 'Come on; let's go and get a cab, go home.'

They walked outside, but then Clare gave an exclamation of dismay. 'I can't go to the flat; I've locked myself out.'

Jack smiled. 'Don't worry, we'll go to my place.' He put his good arm round her. 'I'll take care of you.' And so, for the first time in his life, Jack Straker took his family home.

Later that evening, when they had eaten a meal that Clare had prepared, they had a hilarious time bathing Toby, who was full of excitement at the prospect of them all being together. When they put him to bed in Jack's spare bedroom, he held Clare's hand and said, 'Will Mr Straker always be my daddy?'

'Always,' Jack assured him, his heart wrung. 'There's no getting rid of me now.'

'I don't want to get rid of you,' Toby assured him solemnly. 'I *want* you to be my daddy. But I didn't like it when you were fighting,' he added on an anxious note.

'We weren't really fighting,' Jack explained. 'But I'd been naughty, and Clare was telling me off.' And he grinned at Clare over Toby's head.

'She doesn't kick me when I've been naughty,' Toby pointed out with typical male logic.

Jack ruffled his hair. 'Ah, but you're different. You're special.'

Toby grinned. 'Will you be special now?'

It was Clare who, smiling at Jack, said, 'Oh, yes. Very special.' She got to her feet. 'Why don't you read your son a story?'

When Jack came into the bedroom some time later, she had showered and found one of his shirts to wear as a nightdress. Her hair was a soft, dark cloud and her face was made beautiful by love and happiness. When he looked at her he gave a long sigh. 'You look as you did the first time we ever made love. You were wearing an old shirt of my father's then. Do you remember?'

'I'm surprised you noticed me at all.'

Coming forward, he put his arm round her. 'Oh, I'd noticed. More than noticed—although I'd tried very hard to ignore it. Even to the point of being cold towards you. And, I have to confess, my love, that I wanted you even then. But I fought it off, because you were vulnerable and under my care, and because I was married, and because it seemed all wrong when my father was so ill. But since I met you again—well, it seems to me that he must have been there that night, encouraging us, and I like to think that something of his spirit passed on to Toby, will live on in him.'

Clare smiled, enchanted by the thought. Then she reached up to undo his shirt. 'I think maybe it's time to give you some of that tender loving care.'

'Yes, please.' He kissed her neck.

'Now, don't get any ideas,' she warned. 'You have a broken wrist, remember?'

'It's only my left wrist,' Jack pointed out. 'And a man can do a great deal with only one arm.'

And so he proceeded to prove, to the great satisfaction of them both.

Take 4 bestselling love stories FREE

Plus get a FREE surprise gift!

HARLEQUIN WOMEN KNOW ROMANCE WHEN THEY SEE IT.

The Gentleman & THE HELL RAISER

Don't miss these captivating stories
from two acclaimed authors
of historical romance.

THE GENTLEMAN by Kristin James
THE HELL RAISER by Dorothy Glenn

Two brothers on a collision course
with destiny and love.

Find out how the dust settles October 1997
wherever Harlequin and Silhouette
books are sold.

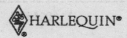 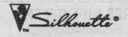

As Seen on TV!

Free Gift Offer

With a Free Gift proof-of-purchase
from any Harlequin® book, you can receive
a beautiful cubic zirconia pendant.

This stunning marquise-shaped stone is a genuine cubic
zirconia—accented by an 18" gold tone necklace.
(Approximate retail value $19.95)

Send for yours today...
compliments of ⬧ HARLEQUIN®

To receive your free gift, a cubic zirconia pendant, send us one original proof-of-purchase, photocopies not accepted, from the back of any Harlequin Romance®, Harlequin Presents®, Harlequin Temptation®, Harlequin Superromance®, Harlequin Intrigue®, Harlequin American Romance®, or Harlequin Historicals® title available at your favorite retail outlet, together with the Free Gift Certificate, plus a check or money order for $1.65 U.S./$2.15 CAN. (do not send cash) to cover postage and handling, payable to Harlequin Free Gift Offer. We will send you the specified gift. Allow 6 to 8 weeks for delivery. Offer good until December 31, 1997, or while quantities last. Offer valid in the U.S. and Canada only.

Free Gift Certificate

Name: _____

Address: _____

City: _____ State/Province: _____ Zip/Postal Code: _____

Mail this certificate, one proof-of-purchase and a check or money order for postage and handling to: HARLEQUIN FREE GIFT OFFER 1997. In the U.S.: 3010 Walden Avenue, P.O. Box 9071, Buffalo NY 14269-9057. In Canada: P.O. Box 604, Fort Erie, Ontario L2Z 5X3.

084-KEZR